I0523973

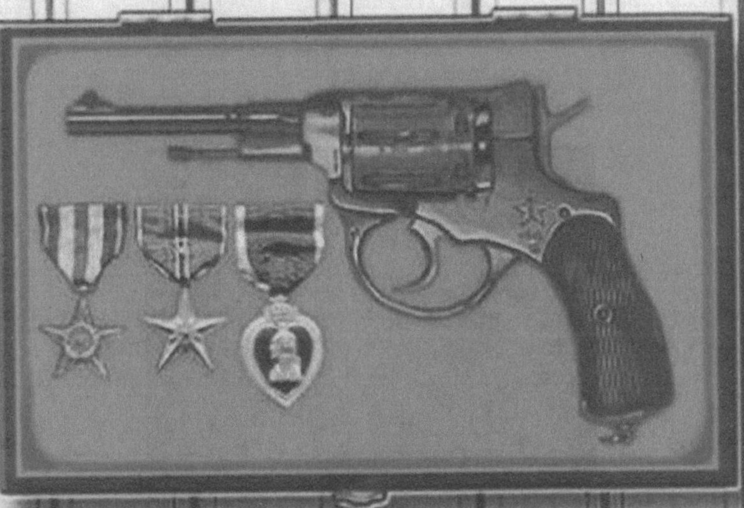

SOUVENIRS

SOUVENIRS

by

Marsha Hinton

ISBN 978-0-9882036-0-0
Published by
Marsha Hinton
DBA New Meadows Media
PO Box 535
Lewiston, ME 04243-0535
United States of America

writer@marshahinton.com

SOUVENIRS

Chapter 1

The convoy of Army mail trucks made its way along the road to Forward Operating Base Fenty.

"Looks like we're going to pick up your boyfriend," Elpidia Delmar said. "Isn't Gabe's team out here doing their thing, whatever that is?"

"He's not my boyfriend," Kara Dyer shot back. Her lips thinned as she glared hard at the road.

"Uh-huh," Delmar grunted. She looked out the truck's passenger side window through the swirling dust.

"So, Dyer, you going to re-up?"

Kara's right hand flipped off the steering wheel as she shrugged.

"Not sure."

"Thought you wanted to go home to that lake of yours."

Kara cast a sharp glance toward the soldier.

"Actually, it's not my lake."

"That's not how it sounds to me. You talk like it's your private lake." Amused at Kara's response, Delmar grinned.

Kara returned to glaring at the road.

"Dyer ancestors have been living around Wea Lake

for a very long time, but we don't own it."

"So, you going to go back to it?"

Kara's eyes darkened. She could remember every detail of where she was on that morning in September. Her decision to drop out of school and join the Army had been made before the day was done. "Eventually. Right now I'm still angry about the whole 9-11 attack. The bad guys are still out there."

Delmar leaned back, rolling her eyes. "Uh-huh."

Kara frowned into the side-view mirror. She could almost see the lake shimmering behind the dust clouds kicked up by the trucks. She thought, "It's not a very big lake; if someone isn't there keeping it healthy, it will die. Pops is getting old."

She recollected how the lake called to the people living around it when even the air perspired in the Indiana summer. Soothing breezes beckoned when the heavy, hot air made it difficult to breathe. Right now she could almost feel the wind blowing off the lake, almost see the refreshing water lapping at her toes before her thoughts were jerked back to the dust and heat.

The chatter on the radio alerted Kara to an approaching motorcycle.

"Which side? Where are they?"

Leaning forward to get a better look in the passenger side-view mirror, Delmar said, "I can't see it. It must be on your side."

Kara's eyes flicked from her side mirror to the road in front of her.

"There. No, I've lost them. Where are they?" Kara demanded.

Chapter 1

"Coming up on this side. Weaving between the vehicles. You should be able to see it now."

"Got it."

The motorcycle was three trucks back. "Probably nothing," Delmar remarked.

Kara ignored the comment as she watched the motorbike's leisurely pace quicken. The driver leaned into the dust kicked up by the truck convoy. She could see him gunning the bike. Moving past Kara's truck, the motorcyclist fumbled with a backpack and tossed it onto the lead vehicle.

"Piper, they threw a satchel onto your--" Kara barked into her headset. As the backpack exploded, the lead truck pulled to the side, taking evasive action.

Kara could see the smoke trail of the RPG before she heard it. Endless hours of combat training took over as the small arms fire pinged off the truck. She automatically reacted to repel any attack from the front by pulling around the lead truck.

Angling to a stop in front of the burning vehicle, Kara's sharp eyes watched the truck convoy from the side-view mirror. Barely noting the movement, she saw Delmar rolling out of the truck's passenger side. Kara glanced at the burning vehicle briefly before turning to fire on the insurgents. Using the smoke as cover, she moved toward the wounded soldiers.

The only thing Kara remembered for months afterward was someone yelling "Medic!" and Gabe's slate-gray eyes before she seemed to slip under the waters of the lake into unconsciousness.

Chapter 2

At the hospital in Germany, the Army gave Kara a medal and told her she was a hero. She didn't feel like a hero; she felt like damaged goods.

The shrapnel that had taken her lower right lung is what ultimately sent Kara back home to Monroe, Indiana. The burn scars ran down her right side from her collar bone to above her thigh, with the shrapnel scar arcing around from her front to her back. As she learned to manage her constant pain, the nightmares became less frequent. The Veteran's Administration provided help with everything from physical therapy to readjustment to civilian life. Despite the support, Kara still felt disengaged. The VA didn't seem able to find a way to make her fit back into her life. For the first time in her life, Kara was adrift.

Sitting on the edge of the dock, Kara leaned back. Her toes explored the ripples washing against the dock. While most of the town still slept, Kara kept this predawn appointment each morning. It provided her a moment to collect the perfect silence around her as armor against the confusing clamor of life.

From the house came the scrape of a chair moving across the kitchen floor, fracturing the silence. Her chin

Chapter 2

dropped to her chest in disappointment. She needed to go to work. Her mom was already at the diner preparing for the folks arriving soon for breakfast.

Grimacing, Kara pushed the lake's whispered promise aside as she grabbed the edge of the dock to rise to her feet. Still listening as the lake called out to her, she lingered, suspended over the sanctuary of the water. One last kick and crisp breeze before another hot summer day began.

The protesting whistle of the tea kettle replaced the soft lapping against the dock. Wincing as the burn scars fought against her movement, she pulled herself upright, her wet feet feeling their way into flip-flops. She straightened her shoulders as she set her face toward the coming day.

Blinded by the overhead lights in the large country kitchen, she took a few moments to adjust her eyes before entering. Her grandfather was eating one of the cream cheese muffins she had baked earlier.

"Stop that!" Kara ordered.

Harold Dyer grinned at his granddaughter then offered her a steaming cup of tea.

"You know Mom is expecting six of those."

"I think I'll finish this one. I don't think Gennie wants to offer half-eaten muffins to paying customers," he answered, winking as he took another bite.

Kara's lips pursed as she opened the oven door. She stepped aside to let the heat escape before taking out the next batch. The warm aroma of blueberry muffins cascaded throughout the kitchen. Her quick eyes scanned the containers waiting for transport to the diner. Except for

Souvenirs

the cream cheese ones, they appeared to be undisturbed. "Good thing you only took one," she commented.

With another wink, Harold nodded toward the steaming muffins and answered, "You might want to look again. I think there are two missing."

Her scowl melted into a mischievous grin. Kara grabbed one of the apple muffins and took a bite. Pulling her chair up next to him, they ate the muffins and watched the night dance with the dawn.

Harold helped Kara take the remaining muffins to the ancient blue station wagon. Harold settled the last box of muffins in the back and closed the hatch. Kara turned to give him a quick hug. "See you later, Pops." She kissed him on his scruffy cheek as he tugged on her pony tail.

As Kara walked around the Ford wagon inspecting the vehicle, a faint smile pulled at Harold's mouth. The habits that had been drilled into her by the Army still held. Climbing behind the steering wheel, she coaxed the old wagon into life. Harold watched as Kara turned onto the gravel road to head for her mother's diner.

Chapter 3

Wes Parkmen, the cook at the Yellow Dog Diner, walked out the back door when he heard the old Ford. "'Morning, Kara. How many you got?" Wes asked while wiping sweat from his bald head.

"These three boxes are all," she said.

"Thanks for doing this. Someone should be down from Fort Wayne today to fix the oven. I keep telling your mom to get a new one."

Kara handed him the boxes then closed the tailgate. She hesitated as she turned east to face a sky already the color of coral. "Looks like it's going to be a hot one today," she said.

Wes squinted into the rising sun, awakening the abundance of laugh lines around his eyes. "Looks that way. I'm real excited about having to slave over a hot stove today." Wiggling his eyebrows, he added, "You want to spend the day with a hottie?"

Her laughter rippled through the still morning air. "How could I refuse such an appealing offer?"

Geneva Dyer was waiting for her father-in-law. Harold had been eating breakfast at the diner for years. This daily ritual was an opportunity to catch up on the latest gossip with the other old men and give a commentary on everything.

It was always entertaining to hear the conversation of the older customers. Kara learned a lot from the massed wisdom; some of it was even true. The gossip proved useful from time to time. She recalled when she was in high school how the old guys had provided a wealth of information about her teachers.

However, the star of the show this morning was her mom. When Geneva laid eyes on Harold, she froze in mid-step. "Pops, why were two muffins missing this morning?" she demanded.

Those close enough to hear paused from eating to stare at Harold. Her head tilted to one side, Geneva placed her hands on her hips as she waited with the sternness of a charge nurse.

Harold sat at the counter, his innocent eyes wide with disbelief.

"Pops!" Geneva barked.

Without taking her eyes off Harold, she shouted towards the kitchen. "Wes, the usual for Pops." She shot one last glare at Harold before stalking toward the register. The listeners relaxed as the performance ended. Geneva smiled at the customer waiting to pay.

"'Morning, Harold." Wes called from the kitchen.

"Good morning, Wes. Another beautiful Hoosier day." Harold clapped his hand on the shoulder of the customer sitting beside him. "Bob, try the cream cheese muffins, they're yummy!"

Geneva's head whipped around. Eyes like lasers locked on Harold as she yelled into the kitchen, "Wes, burn it this time!" The counter erupted with laughter.

Robert Stevenson Hill was a few years younger than Harold. Always solid, Bob had grown rounder as he aged. They were in the same squadron during the Korean War and had been friends ever since. Following Harold back to Monroe, Bob had found a job as a bartender at The Blue Gill Bar and Grill. He purchased the bar when the owner retired, settled down comfortably, and married a local beauty who gave him three sons. He still tended bar most evenings, while his sons had taken over daily operations. Bob rarely missed eating breakfast with Harold.

These two old friends were engaged in an animated conversation as they finished breakfast. At first, the discussion had centered on the effectiveness of the ads for the new deputy. When the discussion segued to the fish shelters built by the Lake Association, their conversation was interrupted.

A thin, sandy-haired man walked into the diner and approached the two men. "Good morning, Harold," he announced. "I knew I'd find you here." Bob elbowed his buddy as Harold became seriously interested in his coffee.

Stan Haley was the local real estate agent, and Kara had known him since grade school. She had never trusted him and felt the hackles go up on the back of her neck as soon as she heard his voice. It was more worrisome that Stan wasn't here to try to flirt with her this time. Kara wondered what he wanted with Pops?

With mischievous eyes twinkling, Harold turned toward Stan and motioned him to take the seat beside him. "Kara, some coffee for Stan, please." he called out.

With ease that came from long practice, Kara

moved across the dining room. "Sure thing, Pops."

Laughing, Wes looked out of the kitchen at Kara.

"What do you think about the fish shelters? Randy has one of those underwater cameras. He said he's going to take some shots for the Association's website," Harold said, nodding at the man who sat down next to Stan.

"Harold, this is Hollis Meyers," Stan said.

"Pleased to meet you, Mr. Meyers. New to Monroe?"

"Hollis is from Washington State," Stan said.

Harold raised his eyebrows. "Welcome to Monroe, Mr. Meyers," Harold looked at Bob. "You here in response to the ad for the deputy job?" He offered Hollis a firm handshake.

Smiling Hollis said, "No. I'm here on a different matter altogether."

"You come from quite a distance, young man. What brought you to our neck of the woods?" Harold asked.

Kara poured coffee for the two men. Stan smiled at Kara as she thought, "He's up to something."

Only Harold's eyes betrayed his enjoyment as Kara forced a smile. "Anything else, gentlemen?"

"I'll be available for lunch later. When do you get your break?" Stan asked.

Bob studied his coffee mug.

"Stan, you know we're busiest at lunch. You're more than welcome to drop in and sit at the counter anytime," she retorted calmly. "More coffee, Bob?"

"What about your old gramps here?" Harold held his cup out.

"Oh, looks like you have plenty there, Pops," Kara beamed. "I think I'll make the rounds with this pot before it

Chapter 3

gets cold. Excuse me, gentlemen."

Kara was on full alert. She kept the counter in sight as she circulated with the coffee. Stop it, Kara, she demanded of herself as she rolled her shoulders and arched her neck to stretch out the tightness that was building. Quit! Smiling, she stooped down to make eye contact with a four-year-old. "Gracie, how are you?" Kara smiled up at Gracie's mother.

"Kara!" The little girl threw her arms around Kara's neck.

"Is Sammy being good?" Kara looked over at the nine-month-old in the highchair.

"No. He hits me with his hammer."

"Hammer?" Kara smiled again at the children's mother as she pulled a plastic rattle shaped like a hammer out of her bag. "Well, we can't have that," Kara said as she kissed Gracie.

Sammy bounced in the highchair until his mother gave him the hammer. He then started pounding it on the table with gusto while Kara attempted to peel Gracie off her neck. "Gracie, I need to give other people some food too, okay? I'll come back later."

Gracie pouted, reluctantly returning to her seat.

"You want some more coffee?" Kara asked Gracie's mother.

Harold's voice rang across the dining room. "Hell, no!" The low murmur of conversation and the tinkling of china abruptly ceased. The only sound was the banging of little Sammy's hammer.

Kara spun around. Bang. BANG. Harold's plate crashed to the floor as his hand swept across the bar. Bang.

Souvenirs

BANG. Geneva jerked away from the cash register. Bob tumbled off his stool. Glaring, he faced Stan.

Bang. BANG. Pops! Kara's large, dark eyes assessed the situation on the other side of the room. Shoving the coffee pot in the geranium planter, she hastened toward her grandfather, skimming around the tables filled with startled customers, all gaping at Harold.

"Stan, what do you think you're doing, asking me to sell my property to a blood-sucking land developer?"

The room was still except for Kara's fluid movements; her full attention on her grandfather.

"Harold, please listen to Hollis. He's as concerned as you are about--"

Harold sent his coffee cup spinning down the counter, splashing its contents on his fellow patrons. "Concerned about making a buck at the expense of the lake? You don't care about this town much, do you? How much you going to get, Stan? What's your share?"

Bob was crouching, his eyes flicking from Harold to Stan. Hollis blanched as he rose from his stool, his eyes tracking between the other two men, apologetic hands offered as a truce flag. "Mr. Dyer, this is not the right time. I only wanted to start the conversation. We can get together at a better time, when you're ready."

Kara noticed the movement. Her gaze shifted to Hollis. She tensed to spring before realizing Hollis wasn't making threatening gestures.

His stool went spinning into Bob as Harold stood up. Stan's face paled as he retreated from Harold's reach. "Turn my land into one of those plastic places where people with more money than sense destroy it? Let some greedy idiot plant putting green lawns? Kill the lake? No! Over my dead body! No!"

Harold spit his words through clenched teeth at Stan. "You know me better than that."

Kara was within reach of Pops as he turned on his heels and stormed toward the door. Geneva had her hand on Bob's trembling shoulders as she talked to him in a low, calm voice, glancing up as Kara closed in on Harold.

"Grandpa, let me take you home."

Angry eyes snapped at Kara as he thrust his arms in the air. "I'm not going home! I'm taking a walk! I can take a walk, can't I?" he barked.

His glare met her dark eyes. Seeing the concern pooled there, he dropped his head. Running his hand through what was left of his hair, he peered at her.

"Grandpa?"

"I'm okay, Little Bit," he grunted. He looked into the face of a woman, but all he saw at the moment was his little girl. "You haven't called me Grandpa in years."

His eyes sparkled as he looked at his granddaughter, still seeing the child. He tugged her ponytail. "I'm okay, Little Bit. Stan always has had the common sense of a tobacco worm. Go back in; your mom will be pitching a fit right about now."

He placed a tender kiss on her brow, his old hand pushing her shoulder as he tried to turn her toward the diner. She wrapped her arms around him. "Pops, are you okay? You spilled your coffee," she said.

He grabbed her pony tail, fiddling with the elastic holding it in place until Kara's silken hair poured out in glinting highlights. His hands were now moving in small, gentle ways. He said, "Spilled it, huh?"

Chuckling, he pushed her away from him so she could see his face. He crossed his eyes. "Scoot or I might explode," he said. Smiling, he cupped her face with his hand.

Kara gave Harold a final searching look. Smiling back at him, she snatched the elastic from his hand. Her smile faded as she looked over her shoulder at the diner.

"Scoot!" He spun her around. As he nudged her toward the door he repeated, "Scoot."

Harold admired the way the sun highlighted his granddaughter's hair until she entered the diner. The tension in her shoulders under the coppery sheet of flowing hair was not missed by the old man. He smiled at her no-nonsense stride. "I almost feel sorry for that boy -- almost." Shaking his head, he walked down the street to the middle of town.

Chapter 4

Kara stopped inside the doorway of the diner, letting the heavy screen door slam behind her. The low hum of contented customers had returned. The bang of the door returned silence to the room. Now all eyes fixed on her. Bob rose as Kara walked toward him. She motioned to him to sit back down with a quick flick of her wrist. He edged back into his seat. Brimming with anger, Kara locked eyes with Stan.

"We need to leave," Stan whispered to Hollis. "Now." He didn't take his eyes off Kara. "Geneva, I'm real sorry about this," he added.

Hollis could feel his heart racing. In spite of the building heat of the day, he felt cold. His mouth opened as his eyes moved from Stan to Kara. He was embarrassed about creating a scene in this very small town. The prospect of establishing a foothold in Indiana through development around Wea Lake was beginning to seem unlikely.

"Kara, I'm sorry. I didn't realize Harold would react so strongly." Stan glanced toward the kitchen. The rear exit was blocked by Wes. "We're leaving now. I promise we won't bother Harold again."

Souvenirs

Kara walked in Stan's direction. Hollis stared incredulously as he watched her approach. Stan's continuous babbling just made Hollis more uneasy as Kara drew closer. She moved with a liquid grace that spoke more of a predator than a beautiful young woman. Her placid expression did nothing to calm him.

Stan jerked his eyes away from her. "Kara, really, we're just leaving." His thinning hair, drenched with sweat, stuck to his head. His eyes darted about as he sought to avoid her. "I'm real sorry." Stan backed toward the counter until its edge bit painfully into his back. Kara stopped about six inches from Stan's face. Alarmed, Hollis stumbled a few steps back.

"Stan, what in the name of my Great Aunt Myrtle was that?" she inquired tersely.

Blinking, Stan tried to push further into the edge of the counter. His pleading eyes sought Geneva, who merely raised an eyebrow. "Kara, we were only asking. I know how Harold feels about development. Mr. Meyers is proposing something I know Harold would consider if he would only listen," he said.

Kara leaned into Stan, somehow avoiding making physical contact. "Really?" she said. Stan made himself very small. Hollis looked toward the door as he considered whether or not he should flee from this angry Amazon.

"Is that so? Pops needs to listen? Looks like he was listening. Seems to me he didn't like what he heard. What exactly about a 'no-development-proposal' upset him so much?"

Hollis took a tentative step toward the door. Not moving from her place in front of Stan, she snapped her

Chapter 4

head around. Hollis shifted uncomfortably under the gaze of those dark eyes, yet held his ground. He thought, *This scary woman just served me coffee!*

"I'm Kara Dyer. Who are you?" she demanded.

Hollis stared at Kara's dark visage, her eyes mesmerizing in their intensity. Those eyes were burning holes in him, leaving him wondering what he'd gotten himself into.

"Kara," Geneva's voice cut through the room, "Could you take this discussion someplace else? The folks here have had enough of a show today."

Kara's eyes took in the dining room in one quick glance, causing most of the customers to make a detailed analysis of their plates.

Geneva's voice became razor-sharp as she addressed Stan. "Pops was right; you do know better."

Kara's eyes moved down the counter where Wes stood waiting by the kitchen exit. Geneva ordered, "Kara, enough!"

Kara's eye's snapped back to her mother. "Stan and you, sir, please join me outside." Turning, she made a slow, sweeping gesture toward the front door. "Gentlemen?" she said.

"Stan, what's going on here?" Hollis hissed. Stan opened his mouth to answer, but quickly closed it as Kara jerked her thumb at the door. Panicked, Stan glanced around for help and found a wall of ice instead.

"Just go along. It'll be alright," Stan whispered to Hollis.

Hollis glared at Stan before following Kara, thinking, *Maybe I can salvage this mess.*

Souvenirs

Kara led the procession to the back of the diner and Wes walked back toward the kitchen. The customer sitting at the end of the counter commented, "Wes, I do believe those two fellows don't have a prayer."

"Not a bet I'd wager on," Wes replied with a grin.

When they reached the back lot of the diner, Kara said,"Well?"

Stan held up his hands, pleading against the wrath facing him. "Kara, we meant no disrespect. I didn't mean to put Harold on the defensive." He put a shaking hand on Kara's arm. She glanced down, but allowed his hand to stay.

"Kara, Hollis has this idea. It's a compelling one that will protect Wea Lake and the woods. He wants to provide decent homes for working families. I honestly believe if Harold would listen, he would like it," he said.

With a violent gesture, she shook off Stan's hand. "This is what you were talking to Pops about? Building a bunch of condos? Do you know what that would do to the lake?"

Stan stepped back as the torrent erupted from Kara. She turned her intense scrutiny on Hollis, all the while realizing this stranger had no idea of the dynamics surrounding him. She took a deep breath. Her words came slowly. "I'm sorry, Mister. Stan has misinformed you. My grandfather will not sell, especially to a land developer," she said.

She turned her gaze on Stan. Stan shifted to a position behind Hollis, nudging gravel around with his foot. "Furthermore, I grew up with Stan. Around here we all know better than to get involved in one of his real estate schemes." She glanced at the cowering Stan then looked

Chapter 4

toward the horizon as she struggled to bite off the words that rushed to her tongue.

"Mister, you don't know, so let me enlighten you. Stan here is always trying to grab the brass ring. Problem is he doesn't know when to stop. If he figures he can make money, he loses all connection with reality. Once again he's moved too fast in the wrong direction to try to make a buck. I'm sorry to say, he's taken you along for the ride."

Right now she wanted to stomp on Stan, getting great satisfaction from the image of him falling to the ground like a wet dishrag with one hit. Part of her realized that smacking Stan wouldn't accomplish anything other than making her feel better. It was almost worth it. "Stan, did you really think this would work?" she asked.

Not waiting for his answer, Kara turned her back on the two men in a complete about-face. Without looking back, she walked toward the rear of the diner; her hair billowing out like a flaming veil behind her.

"Hollis, if you --" Stan started. Hollis held up his hand. He walked away before Stan could finish.

Kara marched back into the diner and punched a pan hanging on a hook over the hot-top, making it clatter against the others as it spun. While she watched the pan jump and dance, she flipped her hair back into a ponytail. Raising his eyebrows, Wes reached up to stop the spinning pan. "Looks like today has more heat in it than just temperature," he said.

Geneva had seen to it that Bob was okay before she walked into the kitchen in time to observe Wes stopping the spinning pan. Ignoring him, she focused on her daughter.

Kara had gained a reputation for a hair-trigger

Souvenirs

temper. Her sense of justice had manifested itself in violent behavior even as a small child. Her second grade teacher, Mrs. Carver, had cited, "developing social awareness" as Kara's biggest need. The same teacher had repeatedly pointed out Kara's need to control her temper.

Geneva knew her daughter and was mindfully aware that Kara's "hair trigger" was initiated by injustice. Like Nemesis, Kara couldn't stop herself from sweeping in to avenge a wrong. Geneva considered this core aspect of Kara's personality to be a positive thing. The struggle had always been in directing her wrath.

She had worked diligently to help Kara cool her fiery temper and use it in productive ways, but nothing she had tried had been as successful as the discipline of Kara's military training. Still, any attempt to control Kara's anger was out of the question once the blood was in the water. It would drive her until the wrong was avenged.

As always, Geneva understood her daughter in a way that Mrs. Carver didn't. Kara needed a well-defined focus that would allow her to blow off steam, such as a physical task or exercise.

"Kara, where's Pops?" Geneva said.

"He walked towards town and must still be there; his truck's still out back," Kara answered. Kara watched the worry lines crease her mother's forehead. "I'll go find him, Mom, don't worry."

"Thanks, baby. Why don't you start at the post office?" Geneva suggested.

Kara waved to her mother as she walked toward the door. Geneva stretched her arms out to relax her shoulders.

"After that big blow-up, we could both use a

Chapter 4

back-rub. How about it?" Wes winked, presenting his back to her. Geneva gave him a look before returning to the dining room. Everything would be okay. She turned to smile at the couple waiting at the cash register.

As Kara walked toward town in search of her grandfather, she could see the air rippling with heat and distorting the buildings in the distance. She turned toward the lake at the group of stores on the south side of the intersection where Route One met Lakeshore Drive. Businesses gave way to homes closer to the lake, with a small group of stores on Lewis Street close to the lake.

She moved methodically down the street looking in the windows of Maury's Barber Shop, The Monroe Herald, and the post office. Kara walked by Dottie's Ice Cream, The Blue Gill, and Vern's gas station. As she approached Walt's Bait and Tackle, she heard Pop's voice and the laughter of old men.

Walking into Walt's, she waited a moment in the entrance to adapt to the dark interior of the store. She saw her grandfather standing at the counter, regaling Walt's customers with the story of his early morning encounter at the diner. Several locals stood around laughing as Pops mimicked Stan. Kara knew the story would grow until even Pops wouldn't recognize it by nightfall.

Since The Blue Gill didn't open until late afternoon, either Walt's bait shop or Maury's barber shop was where the old guys hung out. Enthralled by the story Harold was weaving, the group didn't notice Kara entering the store. Smiling, Kara listened as Harold told his tale. Satisfied he was okay, she decided to just leave without interrupting.

"Hey, Kara, what are you up to? Is Geneva sending

in the troops?" Walt remarked.

"Nope, just making sure Pops wasn't throwing coffee all over town," she quipped.

The old men busted up with laughter while Harold waved his coffee cup around in the air, eyes twinkling.

"Spilling Geneva's good coffee is a reason for some concern, I'd say. Come help yourself to a cup of mine. You can verify Harold's latest saga," Walt said.

The group laughed again.

"Walter, what I told you is the absolute truth," Harold said.

"Thanks for the offer, Walt, but I need to get back to the diner to get ready for lunch. Can you keep this old coot from hurting anyone?" Kara said.

"Can't guarantee that one, Miss Kara," Walt replied dryly.

Kara moved back up the street. She knew Monroe and Wea Lake was like it was the back of her hand. She was born and raised here. She stood and looked around her at the shops and houses of the small town. It was all so familiar and yet so alien. She used to dream of the day when she could live in a more exciting place. Now all she wanted was something, anything to anchor her here. There was a hole inside of her that she couldn't seem to fill.

Kara stopped by the post office on her way back down the road to collect the mail. She immediately recognized several letters with precise block handwriting. An almost electric tingle spread through her as she ran her fingers across the envelopes. She noted the numbers on the lower left-hand corner of the envelopes were out of sequence. There was a gap. She would have to wait to read

Chapter 4

the last two until the missing letter arrived. Stepping back outside, she slipped a fingernail under the fold of one of the envelopes just as she noticed someone coming out of the newspaper office.

"Kara? Is that you? Kara Dyer? I can't believe you're still in this backwater. Look at you! You look fantastic! You must spend hours at the gym."

She tilted her head to one side, considering this newcomer. Pursing her lips, she tried to place the well-dressed young man walking toward her.

"Yeah, I'm Kara Dyer."

"You don't remember me, do you? I can't believe you've forgotten me." Coming toward her, she saw his face break into a dazzling smile as he shook his head in astonishment. "Let's see. Do you remember the time you were about nine? Remember we got stuck on the island when the boat drifted off? I was going to be the hero who rescued the fair maiden and swam off for help on my trusty inner tube. I was half-way to shore when you swam right past me, towing the boat. Not much of a rescue!"

A flashing grin came over Kara's face as she recognized her old friend. "Mike! Yes, I remember that."

"Even at that young age you didn't need a hero. I was so upset," Mike Olson responded.

"We could have waited it out. Someone at my grandfather's would have seen us," she said.

Mike wagged a finger at her. "Now don't go ruining my fondest childhood memories. I always thought no one knew about Indian Island. It was like we were invisible when we were there. No one could see us. It was Neverland," Mike insisted.

Souvenirs

He took Kara's free hand. "What a joy to see you."

Kara warmed at his touch. "You have changed a bit. I like it. When did you get back in town?"

"Oh, I've been in the area a couple of days; almost a week now. It's been a few years since we've hooked up," he said.

She smiled. Mike had been a beautiful boy and had matured into a handsome man. His bright eyes still held the same impish laughter she remembered.

"I heard you were in the Army or something crazy like that," he said.

"Was. I'm out now. Back to working at Mom's place. Why don't you walk me down there? I'll give you a cup of coffee on the house," she teased.

"Oh," Mike grimaced, "I need to get a rain check on that. Where are you staying? You're not still living at Harold's are you?" he said.

"Yeah."

"Oh. Well," Mike frowned "I guess Harold won't eat me. Chances are he's too old to catch me now. Still full of vinegar, isn't he." he said.

Mike's smile was as captivating as she remembered. "Oh, you know Pops," she said.

He glanced down at the phone in his hand as it rang. "Need to get this. I'm trying to drum up more advertising for The Herald. Seems they're struggling. I think we need to work to keep it open." He looked down at his phone again. "Made some calls to some contacts I have to drum up business. Some of them are calling me back already," he continued, looking at his phone again. "Let's get together so we can catch up. I'm living in my grandparent's old place,

Chapter 4

so we're neighbors." He winked at her as he turned to walk away. "Maybe we can go to The Blue Gill tonight. We can create a scandal!"

A smile played around the corners of Kara's mouth. She placed the unopened letter with the other mail. "Sounds good! Give me a call. Do you remember the number?"

With the phone at his ear, he winked and gave her a thumbs-up as he turned the corner.

Chapter 5

Pleasantly preoccupied by her conversation with Mike, she didn't notice the person sitting in his car on the street in front of the diner. Hollis Meyers had returned to his vehicle to regroup, but when he saw Kara striding toward the diner, he threw open the door and jumped out right in front of her. He had hardly set foot on the sidewalk before Kara had him pinned to his car. She had one hand behind her back on her pistol.

Now Hollis was beginning to understand Stan's fear of her. With his heart beating wildly in his chest, his first impulse to fight back passed as he looked into her dark eyes.

"Ms. Dyer, please, I didn't mean to startle you. I was the guy with Stan this morning."

Kara blinked, recognizing who it was. She pushed her weapon back into its holster. "What do you want?" she asked, stepping back.

Hollis raised his hands in surrender. "Ms. Dyer, I'm not going to try to convince you now, and I know we didn't do all that well earlier. Approaching your grandfather the way we did was a mistake," he paused to gauge Kara's reaction. "I would like another opportunity to speak with

Chapter 5

your grandfather about my idea," he broached, his voice steady despite the beating of his heart. He struggled to keep his voice level and his gaze fixed on Kara. Encouraged by the fact she was still listening, he took a deep breath.

"If your grandfather would hear me out he would see I'm not proposing something at cross purposes to what he's trying to protect. I'm not talking about apartments, or condos, or million dollar estates. I'm talking about affordable single family homes, decent housing for the working man." Hollis grabbed a pen. Pulling a piece of paper from his pocket, he scribbled a note. "These are some phone numbers for some of my construction projects. Please contact them. My developments aren't about destroying the environment. In many instances, projects I've developed are actually better for the environment. This proposal might even improve the health of Wea Lake's ecosystems," he added. He offered the note to Kara.

She raised her eyebrows. Relaxing her stance she said, "Mister, you need to sell Pops on that. The show you put on this morning is going to make that nearly impossible. I'm sorry. Stan shouldn't have put you in this position. You seem honest enough, but Pops isn't interested in development, and I'm not either. Sorry." Kara turned to walk away when Hollis reached out, his fingers barely missing her arm. She looked down at the powerless hand attempting to block her way.

"Ms. Dyer, please wait. I know you're extremely unhappy with me right now. Believe me, I understand that. All I'm asking is for you to allow me to share my thoughts and have a fair hearing before you tar and feather me."

Kara's mouth twitched into a small smile as she

turned back to face Hollis. He's actually serious, she thought as she eyed his economy car. She realized he could be driving something flashy like that red sports coupe sitting next to the wind-up clown car he'd rented. She surveyed Hollis more closely as he stood on the sidewalk in his worn blue jeans, plaid shirt, and scuffed-up work boots.

Without Stan tainting her opinion, Hollis seemed to be a decent guy. She decided she liked him. "Now that's something I hadn't thought about before. I don't think I've ever tarred and feathered someone. It might be fun," she said with an evil grin.

Hollis gave her an anxious look, but Kara's kind laughter broke the tension. "Tarring and feathering might be easier for you than dealing with my grandfather right now," she commented. Sticking out her hand, she added, "Mister, you're not such a bad guy. Let me give you a piece of advice, though. You need to stay away from Stan."

Hollis's face lit up as he took her hand. "Call me Hollis, Hollis Meyers."

Kara put her left hand on his elbow to finish the handshake and studied his face. "Again, I want you to know Pops isn't going to be interested in any kind of development. Do you understand?" Kara said.

Hollis, seeing a glimmer of hope, nodded his head. Kara suppressed a smile at his expression. "I also want you to know that even if I ask him to meet with you, he'll probably say no."

Hollis was almost dancing from one foot to the other as he started shaking her hand again. "Thank you, Ms. Dyer. I understand. I appreciate your help. Thank you. This means a lot to me," he said.

Chapter 5

She raised an eyebrow. "I don't know that I'm doing you any favors here. If Pops agrees to talk with you, how do I contact you?" she said.

Smiling, he quickly scribbled a number on the note. His grin broadened as Kara took it from him. "That's my cell phone," he said.

Souvenirs

Chapter 6

By 3 p.m., the sun was beating down on the country roads causing the tar to bubble up between the cracks in the asphalt. Kara was glad to be out of the heat of The Yellow Dog's kitchen. As always, a refreshing breeze was blowing across Wea Lake. Sitting on the edge of the dock with her feet dangling in the cool water once again, she finally had the time to open her letter. There was comfort in seeing Gabe's handwriting march across the page.

"Kara, I was glad to receive your letter today. Don't worry about feeling as if you need to have your weapon close to you. After my first fire fight, I always had mine within reach, even to the point of going to the head with it. You're not crazy. It will get better." She smiled at the thought of the big Marine taking his gun into the bathroom.

"Everyone has told me it's a little strange when you go back to being a civilian. They tell me you don't feel like you connect with ordinary people anymore, so it turns out you're just normal. Give yourself and everyone else some time. Maybe you can help me adjust when my time comes. As far as what your gut tells you about other people, you should listen to that. You have a real talent for seeing what's there and what isn't. Don't doubt that ability. If you're

Chapter 6

uncomfortable with someone, pay attention. That goes double if it's some real estate agent. I can't see you being the main squeeze of someone like that."

Kara grinned before continuing on.

"I don't for a minute think you're somehow emotionally disabled because of the shrapnel and burns. At the time you were angry. I remember. I was there. You didn't see yourself as a victim then, why should you now? Those of us who know, I guess that includes your family, think you're a hero. I certainly do. You're not defective. It might not have anything to do with you. Maybe it's because you're looking for a real man. Too bad all you have around are real estate men. Did I mention you are actually looking for a manly man?"

Kara laughed, dropping the letter in her lap. She remembered seeing Gabe's worried face looming over her as he shouted, "Medic."

She returned to the letter. "Looks like I may be rotating out soon. Maybe I'll try to find Monroe. I think it's time to show those plow boys what a real man looks like."

Kara paused to think of big Gabe's startling gray eyes, framed by his shining black hair. Oh yes, he was a sight to behold. She took a moment to compare him to Mike, who was beautiful, and Stan who is just oily and unattractive. She sat for a few more seconds before sliding the letter back into its envelope.

She looked across at Indian Island. It was only a stone's throw from Pop's dock. A smile spread over her face as she listened to a group of kids shouting as they attempted to erect a tent. An argument seemed to be brewing. The overgrown island was home to scrubby brush, a few small

Souvenirs

trees, and ancient lilac bushes. In the spring when the wind blew in the right direction, the air carried the fragrance of the lilacs to the mainland. The few trees grew around a tumbledown shack where each generation of Monroe kids had attempted to make dubious repairs. The haphazard construction efforts had kept the building upright for decades. Kara remembered secret meetings and a multitude of important plans hatched there when she was in grade school. As Mike had reminded her, it really was Neverland.

Harold had returned home from his antics with his cronies and had noticed Kara sitting on the dock reading her letter. He waited to let her finish without interruption. When he saw her push the folded paper into her pocket, he approached, saying, "Heard you talked to our Mr. Haley and his developer friend this morning." Wincing, Harold slowly eased himself down beside her on the dock. "Old bones."

Kara put her arm through his. She leaned her head against his shoulder. "I love your old bones." They watched the kids disagreeing about the proper way to erect a tent.

"I remember watching you kids doing the same thing only a few years ago."

Kara remained silent.

"Okay, Little Bit, out with it."

Kara snuggled up closer against him. "Mr. Meyers really wants to talk with you, Pops."

Harold stiffened and his voice hardened. "Kara, I'm not interested in talking to him."

"I know."

They sat in silence for several minutes before Harold patted her head. "Something tells me you think I should."

Chapter 6

"He asked for a fair hearing before we tar and feather him. I think it would be fun to tar and feather someone, but Mr. Meyers is too nice, so let's tar and feather Stan."

Harold chuckled. Kara continued, "I told him the answer would probably be no." She slowly splashed her feet in the water.

"I was thinking of something a lot stronger than just saying no, and I have to say I do like the idea of tarring and feathering Stan. Fair hearing, huh? When that guy asked for that, it must have been what softened you up. Bob said they could hear you yelling clear over in the next county."

"You didn't do so bad yourself. Mom should have charged extra."

Pops laughed. With twinkling eyes, he said, "Well, Geneva has already given me instructions with regard to my future behavior."

"Yeah, me too. She's pretty mad at all of us. We'd better stay on her good side and not even steal any more muffins for a while."

"I like the cream cheese ones best hot out of the oven," Harold pouted. "Too bad the man from Fort Wayne showed up to fix the diner oven today." He slapped his knee. "Okay, if the developer can come tonight I'll talk with him. Make it clear to him I'm not going to let anyone harm this lake. It won't help him that he's using my favorite granddaughter to get to me."

Kara looked at the sparkling lake rippling over her toes and the sunfish flashing beneath the surface. The lake had to be protected. She nodded her head in agreement. "I'll give Mr. Meyers a call. He doesn't seem like such a terrible guy once he's away from Stan."

"Stan makes anyone standing close to him look awful. Always did." Harold looked at the letter in her shirt pocket. "Letter from your Marine?"

"He's not my Marine; just a buddy." Harold didn't say anything. Kara continued, "Oh, yeah, guess who I ran into? Mike Olson. He's moved into his grandparent's old place."

Harold grimaced. "Good old Mikey." He looked at Kara. Shaking his head he grumbled, "Never did trust that kid. Only cares about himself. He made trouble everywhere he went. Made his grandparents crazy. I heard he'd moved in and I hoped it wasn't true. Thought he would sell the place as soon as the estate closed probate. Remember him shooting my dog with his pellet gun? And he was always stealing my rowboat."

Kara grinned. She knew how Pops felt about Mike.

He frowned at her. "I always doubted his story about shooting Rags being an accident. That old dog had too much fur for a pellet to get through anyway. The point is, some spoiled, crybaby kid shot my dog."

Kara leaned against her grandfather. Warming to the subject, Harold continued. "Stealing the rowboat is a horse of a different color. You don't accidentally steal someone's rowboat several times. Is he still a liar? Does he still cry crocodile tears? Always was a crybaby."

Kara's infectious laughter rang out over the stillness of the lake. "Don't know. When I ran into him this morning, he was helping the newspaper get some advertising through some connections he has. He doesn't look like a crybaby now, and he wants to take me to The Blue Gill tonight."

Harold grunted. "The oven repair guy from Fort

Chapter 6

Wayne was saying he's going to take out an ad in the Herald. So that's what old Mike is up to?"

"He was on the phone with someone lining up advertising when I ran into him," Kara said.

Harold groaned, "Well, maybe I should give both Meyers and the crybaby a second chance," he rubbed the top of her head. "I didn't think he had it in him." He tilted Kara's head up to face him. "Bob Hill is one of my oldest and best friends, but it seems like Mr. Crybaby Mike could do a lot better than The Blue Gill Bar to woo the prettiest girl in three counties." He gazed at her, making a real effort to see past the little girl he remembered to the young woman she was today. He thought, Kara has proven she can take care of herself. Shoot, she could take care of herself when she was a little girl.

"Well, I guess you're a big girl now." He scrunched up his face. "You're old enough to make your own decisions about the crybaby," he admitted.

She raised her eyebrows as she smiled, making Harold see how much she looked like her mother. "Pop, you said you'd give him a chance. You're always saying there aren't too many options around here." She poked him in the ribs where she knew he had a ticklish spot.

He flinched away from her. "There'd be even more options back at college."

She sat for a few moments, letting her feet dangle in the water. "Oh, Pops." She scooted closer so she could snuggle up next to him again. "I know."

He put his arm around her and sighed. "Kara, be careful. I know you can take care of yourself, and I will try to give that little snot a chance. Just don't be fooled by a pretty face."

Kara splashed the water with her toes. "Okay, Pops. Now let's talk about tarring and feathering Stan!"

Harold laughed. "We'll have to sneak past Geneva. I know where we can get some feathers and we can get all the tar we need from the hardware store."

Chapter 7

Geneva came out on the dock. "You two going to sit there all afternoon admiring the cattails? Kara, baby, you have a phone call."

It pleased Kara that Mike had called. It had been awhile since she had someone her age to talk to besides Stan. The difference was she liked Mike and the possibility existed that something more than friendship could develop. Mike was certainly easy on the eyes. He had always been blessed with naturally-wavy light brown hair and light hazel eyes framed by long lashes. He was a couple of years older than her. As younger children, they had played together when he was visiting. He often stayed with his grandparents for several weeks during the summer and most holidays.

As a boy, he had lived in the "big city" which made him much more exotic than the boring town boys. She had always looked forward to his visits. By the time he turned fourteen, he had become quite the favorite with all the girls, including Kara. Pops had never cared for Mike. Her parents and grandfather managed to erect barriers to all romantic inclinations the two had toward each other. As a result, she didn't see much of Mike in her high school years. When Kara entered her junior year, Mike started college. As far as she knew, Mike hadn't returned to Monroe until his grandmother's funeral. Now Kara was warmly anticipating the renewal of this old childhood friendship.

The phone call didn't last long. Mike firmed up plans to pick her up at 7 p.m. That would give her time to clean up a little bit. She paused, wondering what she should wear. It had been an extraordinarily long time since she had given her clothes any serious consideration.

"Mom, that was Mike Olson, do you remember him?"

"Sarah Olson's grandson?"

"Yeah, he's living at the old farmhouse now."

"So, why is he calling you?" she asked.

Kara blushed. She started moving things aimlessly around the kitchen table. "He's picking me up about 7 p.m. We're going down to The Blue Gill."

"Really," Geneva said. She was glad Kara was finally starting to interact with people her own age. "Well, I'm glad you're going out. At least it isn't Stan." She placed her hand over Kara's. "So, honey, what's the problem?"

Kara blushed an even deeper red. "What do I wear?"

Geneva laughed. "Come on, let's have a look at what's available."

Kara followed her mother into her bedroom. "Oh, I need to call Mr. Meyers and set up a time for him to come over," Kara said matter-of-factly.

"What? That man with Stan this morning? Why?" Geneva stopped rummaging around in the closet.

Kara laughed. "Because he asked nicely."

Geneva's eyes narrowed. "Does your grandfather know you're going to invite that man here?"

Chapter 7

"Yep. I asked Pops and he said it was okay."

Geneva looked genuinely concerned. "Really? You're getting soft, sweetie. You always did have the men in your life wrapped around your little finger. Well, if we're having company, I guess I'd better make a pie."

Geneva returned to examining various options in her closet. Pausing to study Kara with a practiced eye, she pulled out a colorful fitted blouse, saying, "What about this shirt with a pair of nice jeans and these heels? Do you have a nice pair of jeans? You could wear your hair down and put on a little makeup."

Frowning, Kara took the shirt from her mother. She put it back in the closet, selecting one that wasn't so fitted.

"Honey, wear the other shirt. Your scars won't show through; I promise."

Kara's hand went to her right side. "I know they won't show," Kara snapped, "I just like this one better."

"Baby, they won't." Geneva gently took the shirt from Kara. "And leave that gun at home."

Kara crossed her arms as she sat down on her bed.

"Kara, don't shut down. You asked for my help."

She sat on the bed beside Kara. "Baby, I hurt every time I see you wince. Those scars aren't who you are. You certainly shouldn't ever be ashamed of them. You got those scars saving lives. Those scars show the world you're a hero."

Kara's barely perceptible flinch didn't go unnoticed. Biting her bottom lip, Geneva placed her hand on Kara's leg, feeling her stiffen under her touch.

"Kara, it's true."

Geneva sat, allowing stillness to take the moment until Kara relaxed. Her heart felt like it was going to break as she watched her daughter.

Kara's head dropped. "I just don't feel like any kind of hero."

Geneva nodded. "You have a keen awareness that has always stood by you, Kara Dyer. I don't understand why you can't apply it to yourself. No one else thinks that. You were willing to stand in the gap. You didn't think twice about helping others. This is the story your injuries tell. We're so proud of you."

Kara leaned into her mother. Geneva gratefully and gently wrapped her arms around her little girl.

When Geneva opened the door, Hollis stood there with a backpack slung over one shoulder and balancing several long paper tubes under his arm.

He took a deep breath. "Good evening. You probably remember me from this morning." He looked at the abundance of materials he carried. "I'm hoping to talk with Mr. Dyer. Kara called to tell me I could drop by tonight." He smiled shyly.

Geneva stepped aside to allow him to enter. "I'm Geneva, Harold's daughter-in-law. I would ask that you try to avoid a repeat of this morning."

Hollis blushed. He felt like a school boy facing an extremely severe teacher. "I have to apologize for that. It didn't go the way I'd hoped. If I had known Mr. Dyer would react so strongly, I never would have permitted Stan to approach him that way."

Geneva smiled, "Well, now you know more about Stan than you did this morning. I can't hold that against you," Geneva said as she led Hollis into the hallway. "It's a brave man that will face the lion in his own den. I respect

Chapter 7

that. Kara tells me you want a fair hearing." Geneva tapped Hollis's arm, "Let's go sit down in the living room. If you two are going to go at it, you should at least be comfortable. Would you like a glass of iced tea?"

"Ms. Dyer, I have no intention of going at it. I'm so sorry about this morning," Hollis pleaded.

Geneva said, "Well, would you like some iced tea?"

"Yes, thank you." He perched on the edge of the sofa and met Harold's wary eyes. "Mr. Dyer, I am sorry. I had no idea you felt so strongly. Stan said it would be okay to drop in on you at the diner and I followed his advice even though I didn't think it was a great idea. I'm new here, so I relied on Stan's knowledge."

Harold stuck out his hand. "Apology accepted. You couldn't have known. It's not your fault. I only blame Stan." Geneva appeared with a tray and the men took the glasses offered to them before she sat to join them.

Hollis said, "Please don't blame Stan; he was just trying to help me."

"Thanks, Geneva." Harold took a sip of his iced tea. "Well, I do blame Stan. He knows better. It was just flat ignorant of him to put both of us in that position. Sometimes I think there's something wrong with that boy. However, young man, it does speak well of you that you're defending him." Harold paused. "I have to say, Mr. Meyers, not being from around here is not necessarily helping your case."

There was a knock at the door. Geneva watched Kara come down the stairs to answer it.

Hollis took a sip from his glass then adjusted the coaster before setting the glass on it. "Mr. Dyer, I am a developer, but I'm not the kind you described this morning."

Harold raised his voice. "Mr. Meyers, a developer is a developer is a developer. Money hungry thugs who don't give two cents for local ordinances. Going around building million dollar summer palaces where they don't belong. Taking perfectly beautiful countryside then turning it into expensive cookie cutter big boxes that ultimately destroy the environment. The lake would turn into a dead swamp in no time."

Kara opened the door to greet Mike. They both turned their heads at Harold's loud, angry voice coming from the living room. Mike looked at Kara, a question in his eyes.

"It's a continuation of this morning's conversation between Pops and a land developer," Kara explained, taking a quick look into the living room. "Let's leave; Mom's on hand to do damage control." Kara quickly led the way outside where she could still clearly hear the voices through the opened windows.

Hollis said, "I understand, Mr. Dyer, honestly I do. Please just take a moment to look at this sketch plan. It will give you a better explanation than I ever could."

Harold's angry voice responded. "What makes you think I want to look at a bunch of houses popping up like some disease on the landscape?"

Mike said, "Ouch."

Kara winced. Pops wasn't helping to make her first date with Mike go well. She needed to change the focus of the conversation quickly.

"Is this your car?" They were walking up to the red

Chapter 7

coupe she saw parked at The Yellow Dog that morning. She looked down at the interior, admiring the cream-colored leather seats. She asked, "Were you at the diner this morning?"

Mike looked at her. "Uh, no. But I did park there before I walked to town. Don't want her all dinged up by farm machinery. You don't mind, do you? I don't want it all scratched up; I'm leasing it."

"No, of course we don't mind." Her eyes went to the old Ford family wagon. "With a car like that, I'd be worried about it, too."

"Now that I'm living here I think I'll trade her in. Maybe I'll get me a pickup truck to blend into old Monroe. You know of any rusty old pickups for sale?"

Kara looked again at the coupe. Try as she might she could not imagine Mike driving around in an old pickup. Grinning, Kara turned to him. "A few. How about that little beauty there?" She pointed to the old black pickup her grandfather had driven for years.

Harold's distinct voice drifted from the house, "The septic issues alone would destroy the lake."

"Harold's truck? Your grandfather scares me. I think I would have serious issues driving his truck around. Speaking of which, what's the guy he's yelling at now want, anyway?"

Kara pursed her lips. Glancing at the house, she said, "Believe it or not, Pops doesn't always yell."

Mike's eyes widened as he placed his hand on his chest. "He always yelled at me!" Kara returned his charming smile. With a flourish, he opened the car door.

"He wants to develop some of Pop's land. He wants

Souvenirs

to put up affordable housing or something."

Mike closed the car door as his smiled faded. Looking towards the house, he thought, "Well, I'll be damned."

Chapter 8

The Blue Gill made up for what it lacked in ambiance by keeping late hours. It sold fried offerings such as fish, hamburgers, and tenderloin sandwiches along with a limited selection of "adult beverages." Standing in one corner was a jukebox filled with "classic rock" music.

Kara paused. Her sharp eyes scanned the dark interior before entering. "Takes a minute to adjust your sight to this place, doesn't it? Remember when we kept trying to sneak in here?" Mike remarked.

"You kept trying. I just happened to be standing around once. I remember you got caught that time and I got in trouble for it. As far as I recollect, you never actually got in."

Grinning with perfect teeth he said, "As far as anyone knows."

They opted for a seat at the bar. "After you, my lady."

Kara smiled, selecting a seat at the end of the bar. She settled in with her back to the wall. "Not as exciting as we thought it would be all those years ago." She looked around at the various fish mounted on plaques. The soft lighting did little to flatter the dark, rustic decor. "In fact, it's kind of awful."

Souvenirs

"True, true." Mike glanced around. "You class up the place, though. You're absolutely stunning." He pushed aside the condiment tray on the counter. "I don't think the folks in Monroe would know what to do with a fine restaurant. Come to Chicago with me next time I go. I'll take you someplace where you belong."

Quit panicking! Say something, dummy! Kara thought. "I might take you up on that. Been a while since I went to Chicago," she said. "Maybe we could catch a Cubs game."

Mike brushed her hand with his. "Excellent. It's a date. I'll be the envy of every guy in the city."

Kara studied Mike to see if he was teasing. A mischievous grin played at the corners of his mouth. Blushing, she snatched up a menu, examining it before flicking off a stray bit of mustard.

Mike brushed her hand with his again, lingering a few seconds. As Kara looked up into his eyes, he said, "You are beautiful." As he brushed a strand of hair from her face, she forced herself to remain still as he took her hand. A gentle warmth spread over Kara. Time seemed suspended in that moment.

"You know what you want or should I give you more time?" the waitress asked. Kara visibly jerked at her sudden appearance. She caught herself reaching for the gun she left at home. Mike held fast to her other hand, puzzled by her odd movements.

Kara fought her immediate response, which was to make him let go. She didn't need to get into a tugging contest in the middle of a local bar. Guess Mom was right about the gun. I don't want to shoot up The Blue Gill, she

Chapter 8

thought as she forced herself to go through the relaxation exercises the doctor at the VA had taught her.

Mike's bemused eyes stayed on Kara as he ordered for the two of them. "We'll take two fish sandwich baskets with fries."

The waitress went on before Kara mumbled, "I'll take my hand back now." She didn't look at Mike.

He tilted his head, frowning before squeezing her hand and letting go. "Sorry. Are you mad at me?"

Kara said, "No, it was a little bit awkward; that's all," she said, "I was thinking about ordering the tenderloin basket."

"Oh! Sorry. I can change the order if you want."

"No, the fish basket is fine."

She nervously moved the condiments around on the bar. Why am I being so snippy with him? she thought.

Mike cleared his throat. "Why did you go into the Army?"

"Oh, it seemed like the right thing to do at the time. I'd started my third year at school when the terrorists attacked. I got mad and enlisted the next day."

"Sounds like you. Little-miss-take-charge; the hero off rushing to the rescue; the masked ranger riding in to save the day; treading-where-angels-fear-to-tread kind of girl." His smile washed over her, "It must not have worked out. They gave you a humdrum job or you must have got bored because you're not in anymore, am I right?"

"Something like that." Kara organized the colored packets of sweetener.

"Are you going to finish school?"

Her embarrassment was fading as Mike pulled her

into the conversation. She studied him before returning his smile then looked down at the counter. "Maybe, I don't know. College was okay, but I'm not sure what direction I'm going in. Until I figure that out, it seems kind of silly to spend the money." Kara wrinkled her nose. "I'm a little bit older than most college kids. Mom, Pops, everybody wants me to go back. My brother is about done with med school. He keeps pestering me to finish my degree." Kara centered the salt shaker on the counter.

"Your folks are right. I want you to go back, too. You should complete your degree. Beauty and brains are a knock-out combination in my book. You shouldn't waste either."

Kara blushed, "You look good, too. What have you been doing with yourself?"

"Oh, school. Then work in the cold city." His impish grin flashed at her. "I'm in investing. Even before my grandparents passed on, I thought I'd move down here." He straightened up. "I'm going to hang my shingle out in old Monroe. Investing and telecommuting go together like peanut butter and jelly. They're made for each other. Monroe has always been home to me and I'm not so far away I can't go up where the action is. It'll be nice to tone it down a bit."

"You're an investor? For real? Any good at it? That's a stupid question." Kara glanced out the door. "Look at what you're driving."

Mike smiled as he brushed her hand again. Kara anticipated the contact this time and overcame the urge to pull away. Why is this so hard? It just isn't going all that well. I need to relax, she thought as she started stacking coasters.

Chapter 8

"It sounded this morning like you were in advertising. Were you the one who got the oven guy to buy advertising in the Herald?" she asked.

Mike bit his upper lip and looked down at the counter. Looking back up, he gave Kara an embarrassed smile. "Nope, not in advertising. When I got back to town, I went down to the newspaper. I needed to get the newspaper delivery started back up. I also wanted to run a small ad for my business. When I was in there, I found out they weren't doing so well. They actually said they might have to quit publication. I couldn't let that happen; I have a business to start. I know a few people. In a couple of days, I learned what vendors do business down here. The oven repair guy was one of them. I made some calls; no big deal."

"Wow. That was nice."

Mike grinned. "Oh, not really. I need a local advertising platform for my investing business. Self-interest really."

Kara squeezed his hand. "Uh-huh." She realized she was starting to enjoy herself. "Are you going to stay at the farm house? It seems pretty big for one person even with running a business out of it. There's all that farm land. Pops thought you would sell it all."

"Well, Harold was wrong on that account." Mike momentarily lost his smile. His gaze became unfocused as he stared at his reflection in the mirror over the bar. Kara watched his expression flicker. Curious, she shifted to his reflection as well.

Noticing her motion, he turned back to her. "Sorry. Contemplating business again," he stroked the back of her hand. "It is pretty big. I thought about fixing it up into a

49

couple of apartments. I could rent them out to generate another stream of revenue. I've even contacted some contractors to explore that option. Of course, having my office at the old farm house is going to save me a ton of money." He took her hand again. "You could be my first tenant. I'd make you a deal you can't refuse on the rent. That would certainly solve the empty farm house thing."

Kara tingled. Mike smiled as he watched Kara consider the idea. He wrapped his hands around hers then let them go with a soft pat, returning his gaze to the mirror behind the bar.

Kara moved the salt shaker again. *He looks like he wishes he was anywhere else. I'm so stupid. This is turning out to be a stellar first date,* Kara thought as she again stacked the paper coasters. *Why can't I be normal? He's being so nice to me.*

Something wasn't right. She set the coasters aside, thinking, *What's wrong with me? Why can't I say something interesting? Look at him. He isn't even really here anymore, and if he ever saw my scars, he'd run in the other direction.* She had to say something!

"Mike, look, I'm having a little trouble here."

Mike's eyes lingered on a spot on the mirror. "Huh?"

"Mike, when I was in the Army some stuff happened that has made things difficult for me."

Mike turned to her, concern on his face.

Kara felt relief that Mike was listening. She had been unable to bring herself to discuss her injuries with her family. They didn't seem to treat her differently because of the scars, but she simply wasn't ready to talk to them.

Mike placed a reassuring hand on her arm. "Like

Chapter 8

that Gulf War syndrome or whatever it is? They don't let women go into battle, do they?"

The waitress plopped down the fish baskets. "Anything else?"

Mike looked at his basket, the various layers of the sandwich sliding in different directions. Kara said, "No, thanks." She attempted to pick up her sandwich which shifting around in her hands as if it had a mind of its own. Mike's eyes twinkled as he suppressed a giggle.

They ate in silence for a few minutes when Mike said, "I don't mean to beat a dead horse." His engaging grin sparkled. "I've got to know. When you were in the Army, were you some secret ops warrior princess or something?"

"No. I was a driver."

Smiling, Mike leaned back. "Oh, like convoys and stuff."

"And stuff."

"Stuff, huh?" His soft eyes watched her. He gently took the salt shaker out of her hand.

When the waitress showed up with the bill, Mike reached around for his wallet, flipping it open to pull out a credit card. What caught Kara's eye was the membership card to a gun club. "You're a member of a gun club?"

Mike flipped the card out. "Yep. I guess being in the Army, you know how to handle a gun. Got hooked in my pellet gun days. Don't worry, this club is exclusive, not your regular rabble. I could probably get you in as a member. We could go together."

The waitress returned with the card, "Sir, this card didn't go through." Mike snatched the card back, embarrassed, and pulled a couple twenties from his wallet.

Souvenirs

"Oh, that's right. Changed addresses. Haven't gotten my new card yet," he said. He handed the cash to the waitress, "This should cover it."

Kara glanced at the gun club card as Mike paid the waitress. Maybe they had more in common than she thought.

Chapter 9

The ride home was pleasant enough, with Kara enjoying zooming along the road with the top down. Mike's car purred instead of chugged along like the Ford.

Even while she enjoyed the ride, Kara still felt something was out of place. Looking up at the stars, she was convinced it was her. For some reason, the memory of Mrs. Carver telling her parents she was a square peg in a round hole came back to her. At seven years old, she had wondered what Mrs. Carver had meant.

She watched Mike as he easily steered the speeding car along the road. It had always been difficult for her to be in a situation where she didn't understand the rules. She didn't always get the nuances most people seemed to follow instinctively, and this had become much worse since she had returned home to the lake. It should have been easier here. Again, she thought, it had to be a flaw in her.

The people around Monroe had known her family for generations before she arrived on the scene and they all seemed to accept her at face value. The diner had always been comfortable because she knew the rules there. The Army had also been comfortable for the same reason. The rules were clear-cut and spelled out in black and white.

Souvenirs

As she admired Mike, she realized she wanted to have a good relationship with him. At the very least, it would prove her second grade teacher wrong. She so wanted to be like everyone else. As Kara sat next to Mike in the fast car, she was afraid that somehow the fuel that burned her right side and arm had burned out any remaining part of normal she had in her; that somehow it had burned out her ability to connect at a deeper level with another human being.

Hollis's car was still in the driveway when Mike walked her to the house. As they approached, there were no raised voices. The living room was strewn with curling plot plans, sketches, and stacks of papers. It surprised Kara to hear calm voices coming from the kitchen.

Kara indicated that Mike should follow her. He took a step back towards the living room. "No, thanks!" Mike looked down the hall. "I'll stay here. Your grandfather might throw something at me."

Frowning, Kara followed his glance down the hall. Mike held up a hand. "I already told you, Harold scares me." He looked at the chaos in the living room. "I'll hide in here under all this paper."

Kara shrugged away her disappointment. "Mike's probably right," she thought. "Those two have a pretty rocky history to get past. I don't want this to be my first, and last, date with him."

Kara became even more surprised at the scene she found in the kitchen. There were the remains of what looked like dinner on the table in front of her grandfather, her mother, and Hollis. The three of them were each enjoying hefty slices of Geneva's sugar cream pie. Kara looked quizzically at her mom.

Geneva simply pointed to an empty chair. "Kara, come join us. Did you have a good time?"

"Oh, we had the fish basket at The Blue Gill. Mike is waiting for me in the living room."

Harold grunted as Geneva gave him a sharp glance. "Well, tell him to come in here with us," Harold said.

When Kara went to fetch her date, she saw that Mike had cleared up some of the scattered papers. He was currently looking at the bric-a-brac on the walls. "Mike, gird up your loins and join us in the kitchen."

"Only if you will save me from the raging beast at the end of the hall, oh, illustrious warrior princess."

Kara laughed and turned toward the kitchen. "Mom, Pops, you remember Mike Olson."

"Oh, it's the kid who kept stealing my rowboat. Still shooting perfectly nice dogs are you?"

Mike's smile hardened, but his voice maintained a pleasant business tone. He said, "Hello, Mr. Dyer. I don't accidentally shoot dogs or borrow rowboats anymore."

Geneva glanced at Harold again. Shifting his eyes, he suddenly found his pie to be very interesting. Geneva interjected, "Yes, I remember you, Mike. I saw you at Sara's funeral. It's been a tremendous loss to the community to be without your grandparents.

Mike turned even more sober. "Thank you, Ms. Dyer."

"Come have a seat and have some pie. How long are you in town?

"Oh, I've moved here now. I've been in town just a few days. Mike looked at Hollis.

Souvenirs

"Mike, this is Mr. Meyers. He's a newcomer to Monroe."

"New? Are you planning on settling here?" Mike grinned. "I spent the summers of my childhood here with my grandparents. What brings you here?"

"Call me Hollis. I'm here on business."

"I saw all the plans in the living room. Planning a development?" Mike glanced at Harold.

"We did make a mess in there. Geneva, I promise I'll clean it all up before I leave," Hollis said.

"Are you staying in the area some place? I've got a big old farm house sitting pretty empty right now," Mike said.

Hollis answered, "Thanks for the offer, but I've got a cabin at Indian Rest. It's close and works for me for now."

Mike said, "Indian Rest. A little bucolic for my taste, but it is convenient." Mike smiled. "The commute is a real killer from the closest respectable motel. Well, sorry, but I have to go, I've got an early start tomorrow morning. I'll have to take a rain check on the pie. Thank you, Ms. Dyer. It was nice to meet you, Hollis."

Mike paused at the entrance to the living room to wait for Kara. "Hard to believe Harold is sitting at his own table actually talking to a developer."

"Mike, he's not the man-eating monster you seem to think he is." Kara wrinkled her nose. "But I'm surprised they're still talking. It must be a pretty incredible housing development."

"Obviously," Mike grunted. He frowned as he stuck his head in the living room for one last look. "Harold certainly has mellowed. I see he still keeps that old gun on

Chapter 9

the wall. I'm shocked he didn't shoot Hollis with it on sight. Even seeing it with my own eyes, from what I know about your grandfather, I can't believe he's in there eating pie with a developer. Hell must have frozen over."

Kara pursed her lips before nodding slowly. "It did seem like they were getting along pretty well."

"It did." Mike looked at his watch. "I need to get going. Walk me to my car?" The smile he turned to Kara filled her with warmth. "Makes courting you easier with Harold all mellow. I might even have a chance." Kara allowed him to take her hand as they walked out of the house toward his car.

"Next time we'll go someplace nicer than The Blue Gill. My schedule is pretty tight right now." He moved closer. Almost purring, he said, "Soon. Very soon." He pulled her in to kiss her.

Kara panicked. Relax, you idiot! she said to herself as she ended the kiss abruptly and moved away from him. She could see the disappointment in his eyes and knew the kiss wasn't everything he was expecting. She berated herself. What's wrong with me? Why can't I just enjoy his company? she thought. There was a time when she would have given almost anything to be in this situation with him. Forcing a smile she said, "Oh, The Blue Gill has all that rustic charm, and of course, the company was wonderful." Steeling herself, she initiated the kiss this time. Leaning away from him again she added, "Besides, you have a cool car."

Smiling, he stroked the automobile's hood. "It does get people's attention."

She watched Mike's flashy car turn onto the road before she reentered the kitchen, thinking that Mike was right. Pops should have been yelling then kicking Hollis out. She certainly hadn't expected to see Hollis still here when she returned home. Against all odds, here Pops sat with a developer in his kitchen, actually listening to him. The conversation was animated and everyone was being civil.

Kara return to the house. She could hear her mother laughing and the sound drew Kara back to the kitchen. Geneva looked over her shoulder when Kara entered the kitchen. Smiling she jabbed a thumb in the direction of the two men then pushed a piece of pie over to an empty spot at the table. Kara sat down and picked up a fork.

"Most of the property would remain as it is now," Hollis was saying as he waved his fork in the general direction of the lake. "The lawn area will be kept to a minimum." Hollis placed his fork down before ticking points off on his fingers. "Clustering housing will reduce the need for lawn and allow sharing of resources. There's going to be a central recreational area to provide for green space and restrictions on tree removal. Deed restrictions for environmental protection are part of the purchase agreement for the property owners." Hollis grabbed his fork and stood it upright. "Mature trees that we absolutely have to remove for construction are going to be replaced with six-foot-tall trees."

"Hollis, you can put anything on paper, but how you going to make someone do it?" Pops was stabbing his pie with his fork.

Kara's eyes twinkled as she watched the two men talking. When she finished her pie, she used her fork to tap her plate and get their attention. They stopped talking and turned to look at her. "Mr. Meyers, Pops, Mom, I don't want

Chapter 9

to be rude, but I need to get to bed. I've got to get up early tomorrow and slave away for my cruel boss." She leaned over and kissed her mother's cheek.

Geneva said, "I'm going to bed myself. You know how I've got to stay right on top of things. Seems some of my staff members are slackers." She cleared the plates with Kara.

Standing, Hollis took the plates out of their hands and rinsed them at the sink. "Mrs. Dyer, Kara, I appreciate your help."

"Sneaky of you to win over the one person who has always been able to talk me into anything," Harold growled.

Grinning, Hollis patted Kara's hand as he turned to Harold. "I didn't know that at the time. However, I will keep that piece of information handy." He smiled at Kara. "Harold, I don't think I've been yelled at like that by anyone. You two must be experts."

"You two are not to take that as a compliment. Don't encourage them, Hollis," Geneva said.

The response came together, "Yes 'um."

Kara made her way upstairs and walked to her bedroom's open window. She could see the lantern light coming from the island and hear the soft drone of the voices coming from the kitchen. She fell asleep easily as she listened to the lake lapping against the dock.

Chapter 10

"Mom, I'm not kidding, I believe that global warming is doing a test run here in Monroe." Kara was helping out in the kitchen with the weekend breakfast crowd. She pulled at her sweat-soaked shirt.

"Kara, you could pull off that huge shirt. That tank top looks pretty on you."

Kara touched the scars on her side, thinking about how she'd always been proud of her figure and how good she'd looked in a bikini until she'd gotten burned. Self-conscious about the scars, she always went to extraordinary lengths to hide them. The color rose in her cheeks as she thought about the puckers that now adorned her torso and upper arm.

Geneva regretted the words. She ached to help her daughter deal with her injuries. She also knew she needed to wait for Kara to be prepared to receive that help. Geneva said, "Why don't I bring in another fan?"

Wes saw the pain reflected in both their faces. He remarked, "Oh, I see who you love. Why don't you bring in more fans for me?"

"Wes, you didn't ask."

"Are you telling me I should complain to get what I

Chapter 10

need?"

Geneva shot a glance at him, "Like you don't do enough of that as it is?"

"Right. I've got a kitchen to run here. Kara, cook some onions, will you?" Wes looked over at Geneva and winked at her while Kara started chopping onions.

Harold walked into The Yellow Dog about 10 a.m. and plunked down at the counter. "You're running late today." Geneva said. "Bob was all worried."

"Been making some phone calls. I'm going up to town later to take care of some business. Won't be back for dinner. I'll catch up with Bob later."

"Oh, if you're going that way anyway, let me give you a list of things you can pick up for me. You're taking your truck, aren't you?"

Harold sighed as he thrust his hand out for the list.

It was almost closing time when Stan walked into the diner. He shot a nervous glance at Kara then moved over to the register. "Geneva, do you have a minute?"

"Sure, Stan. Kara, can you cover the register?" Kara's eyes narrowed as she watched Geneva and Stan go to a booth. Stan looked back at Kara before sitting down.

Geneva glanced at Kara then turned her attention to Stan. "What do you need?"

"I've got to know whether Hollis and Harold are working on a deal."

Geneva's blank gaze held Stan's eyes. "That, young man, is none of your business."

Stan ran his fingers through his sandy hair. "I need to know because he is my client."

"Harold did speak with Hollis last night at the

house," Geneva said. "Don't you think you should be discussing this with your client?"

"They talked?"

"Stan, what did you think Hollis was going to do?"

Stan's eyes became unfocused and he became very still. Geneva watched his mouth harden and his eyes refocus. He pushed his way out of the booth and said, "He's going to cut me out."

Kara was giving out change when she saw Stan collide with a customer as he hurried out the door. She turned to look at her mother. Geneva's shrugged and then waved her hand in a dismissive motion at the retreating Stan as she moved toward the register.

"What's up with Stan?" Kara said, "He looked pretty mad. I don't think it's because we ran out of coconut cream pie today."

"He's upset because he thinks Hollis is cutting him out of the development deal. He's probably going to do something dumb."

"Well, what did he think that performance would amount to yesterday? When isn't Stan up to something dumb?" Kara said. "I bet he's going to try to weasel himself into getting a cut somehow."

Geneva threw up her hands. "It's always something with him."

Kara knew Stan well enough to say he'd developed a passion for money as a kid, but being lazy was a colossal roadblock. He was good at coming up with dubious get-rich-quick schemes that never quite worked. For some reason, he'd stayed in Monroe because, she surmised, he knew he'd be lost in the big city. Stan had enough success

Chapter 10

to make a livable income in spite of all his misguided scheming. However, it wasn't the lifestyle that Kara was certain he dreamed about.

Chest tight and heart pounding, Stan walked down the road to his small office. His mind was full of his need to land this deal. Sales had been flat and his checking account needed an infusion of cash fast. He just couldn't afford to let any commission get away. He thought, I need to reel this one in. If Harold didn't go so crazy about protecting the lake, I know I could move more properties.

Jerking the door open, Stan looked around at his tiny office and gave the trash can a good hard kick, thinking, I should have had Hollis sign that contract before we went to talk to Harold. He thinks he's pretty smart using me that way to get to that old guy. Well, I can play that game, too.

Stan glared at the unsigned contract with Hollis sitting on his desk and crumpled it, shouting loudly, "I don't need you." Then he plopped down dejectedly in his chair, thinking, I've got to think bigger.

Chapter 11

The sound of her grandfather's truck pulling into the driveway woke Kara up. She reached under the pillow for her gun. Satisfied it was still there, she rolled over and went back to sleep.

Bob was closing up The Blue Gill about the time Harold was getting home. Most of the patrons had gone, however, one lone customer had lingered.

Mike whined, "Bob, don't say you're closing. I just got here." He leaned across the bar, pleading. "Don't throw me out into the cold."

"Buddy, you need to give me your keys."

"Bob, I can drive." Mike swayed. He stumbled into one of the bar stools and said incoherently, "All I want to do is sit here for a few minutes. I'll be just fine."

"I'll take your keys." Bob walked around the bar and put a hand on Mike's shoulder which the drunken man pushed at ineffectively. "Buddy, you know I can't let you drive home like this."

"It's too far to walk. Can you call a cab? Oh right, we're in little Monroe." Mike giggled and then pouted. "Bobby, where do I go? Can't you stay open? Can't I just stay here? You have a bed in the back somewhere, don't you? Or

Chapter 11

I could sleep on the bar." Mike patted the bar.

"Keys or I'm calling the cops." Mike's smile faded. He puckered up like a child who was about to cry.

"Okay." Mike stood unsteadily. He fished around in his pocket until he found the keys. Giggling, he waved them in the air. "You have to push this button here." With a firm look on his face, Bob held his hand out until Mike dropped the keys in his open palm.

"Wait! Just one more for the road?" Mike spun away from Bob, lurching behind the bar and grabbing at the tap. Unable to hold on to it, he lost his balance, falling to the floor. Bob shook his head and looked at his watch. "Buddy, you can't stay here."

"But I don't want to go!" Mike cried as he fumbled around behind the bar.

Bob went around to Mike. "Come on, let's go. Bar's closed."

He started singing as Bob helped him up and got him to the door. It was all he could do to keep from falling himself.

When they got to the red coupe, Bob had to let go to open the door and Mike folded into a heap on the ground. Bob fumbled with the seat until he found the lever to make it lean back. Mike was dead weight. Getting a bit of a workout, Bob got him back on his feet then pushed him into the car.

"Okay buddy," he said, "you sleep it off here, okay? I'll give you the keys in the morning." Bob grabbed the black coat on the back seat and covered Mike up with it. Making sure he was secure, Bob walked back to The Blue Gill and made a quick check to secure the building. Tossing the man's keys into a bin behind the bar, his eyes squinted as he thought, "That guy is pretty tight; I'd better leave him a note." Bob checked on the sleeping drunk one more time, adjusting the coat and sticking his note to the car's dash. He assured himself, "He'll be okay."

The local police chief, Blake Davis pulled up beside Bob before the turnoff to the Indian Rest Cabins. Bob was putting something in his trunk. "You need any help, Bob?"

"No, Blake. I'm out here rotating my tires at 2 a.m. in the morning, doesn't everyone?" Bob slammed the trunk down.

Blake took a quick look at the tiny doughnut tire on the right rear. "Okay." He pulled away as Bob slammed the car door.

Randy was finishing up his paper route when he spotted someone walking along Lakeshore Road. He slowed to a stop, but the man kept walking. He rolled down his window. "Hey, you want a ride somewhere?" he called out. The figure in the hooded jacket did not pause or turn around. "Buddy, can I drop you someplace?" The person kept walking. Shrugging his shoulders, Randy continued on down the road toward Monroe. The walker fixed the license plate number of the old tan car in his head.

Chapter 12

In her sleep, Kara jerked. The still air over the surface of the lake carried the sound of a gunshot. The distinctive popping noise had intruded into her dreams, wrapping itself around images already burned into her subconscious mind. In Kara's dreams, her hands reached for the wheel of the truck as she relived the day of the attack on the convoy once more. The nightmare's images transported her back to the dusty road in the military convoy as she drove that armored mail truck. Delmar had given her one of her mom's cookies from the care package, as Kara remarked, "It's so stinking hot."

The convoy was kicking up yellow dust that coated everything, the grit working its way into every pore of her exposed skin. The rear passenger on the motorcycle glanced at her as they passed, putting her on full alert. He then tossed a bag onto the lead truck. "Piper, they threw a satchel onto your--," Kara barked as the dream unfolded.

She managed to keep from colliding with the burning truck in front of her, jerking her vehicle to a stop at an angle to the front of the burning lead vehicle. Delmar had her weapon out scanning the area. She heard a whoosh and flinched as the RPG missed the line of trucks. The shell buried itself in the sand beyond the right side of the caravan. Shielding herself from the spray of debris, she slid out on the driver's side, running to pull injured soldiers out of the lead truck. Small arms fire was pinging off the armor of the vehicles. Another explosion sprayed sand everywhere.

Operating on instinct, her training took over as she moved forward, barking orders. She secured the wounded in the most protected area then quickly positioned those who were able to defend the site. There were too few of them, way too few. Delmar turned to her and shouted, "Here they come!" right before she went down. Blood splattered Kara's face.

She moved like an avenging avatar firing her weapon with deadly accuracy. The ragtag insurgents drew back to a protected position. Crack. The blow to her ceramic flak jacket sent waves of pain into her chest, the force of it knocking her down. There was no blood; she was okay. Her temper was raging now; it would take a Mac truck to stop her. She sprang up like a cat, firing her weapon even before she gained her feet. The wordless primitive sounds emitting from her throat were all she could hear.

"Delmar! Delmar!" Delmar moaned as Kara grabbed the wounded soldier's web gear. "Delmar! Stay with me!" Kara pulled Delmar back to the center of the wounded. "Get someone to take care of this soldier!" she barked. Kara returned to firing at the enemy. Something clipped her helmet, making her ears ring. She spun around, running toward the other side. The insurgents were attempting to flank their position.

Crack. They had managed to hit the turret gun, sending shrapnel flying into her vest. She didn't get knocked

Chapter 12

down this time and took a step backwards before bracing her feet. Her shots hit the center of the guy firing at her, dropping him like a rag doll. She kept advancing, almost feral at this point. Her rage had complete control, driving her forward.

Another explosion. Turning away, Kara suddenly felt puzzled over an intense burning in her side. Something hit her chest, throwing her backwards. The lines from the movie she loved as a kid kept playing in her head. I'm melting, I'm melting! She fell in what seemed like slow motion, the rifle slipping from her grasp. She watched the enemy running towards her. "So this is what it's like to die." The words gurgled out in a bloody foam.

She jerked awake, covered in sweat although the air was cool. Her hand moved to her right side to touch the wound. Where am I, she wondered as she reached under her pillow for her weapon, wrapping her hand around the hard metal. She looked around, calming herself. Realizing she was safe in her room at home, her breathing slowed.

The sound of the gun fire in her dream had seemed so real. She put her gun back under her pillow then sat up, wiping the sweat from her eyes. It took her a few more minutes to get her bearings as she told herself she was home.

She rubbed her face and glanced at the alarm clock, realizing she'd have to be up in an hour. Knowing she wasn't going to get back to sleep, she pulled on her jeans and a t-shirt, completing the ensemble with a hooded sweatshirt. She then crept down the stairs, avoiding the creaky boards. She ran water in the kettle and set out a cup for tea.

"Thought I heard you up." Kara's cries had woken

Souvenirs

her mother. Looking at her daughter, she knew it was another nightmare. Her heart ached for her little girl.

Her mother was wearing her Chicago Cubs logo pajamas, which made Kara smile. Geneva noticed the dark circles under her daughter's eyes and the deep lines drawn on her face. Her daughter looked years older than she was. *What in the world made me remind Kara of her scars yesterday? It's been weeks since the last nightmare,* Geneva reprimanded herself as she wrapped her arms around Kara. Kara didn't cry; she just melted into her mother's arms.

Harold walked into the kitchen, letting the door bang behind him. He knew instantly that Kara had endured another horrible dream. He had heard a sharp sound, like a gun shot, and was determined to figure out what it was. He went outside to investigate, finally deciding it was the kids on the island fooling around. He told himself it was probably just firecrackers.

Geneva startled at the slamming of the door. "Goodness, Pops, you almost gave me a heart attack!" Geneva scolded.

He replied drily, "Those pajamas almost gave ME a heart attack! Well, here we all are. Is that the tea kettle I hear?"

Kara asked, "Pops, what are you doing up so early?"

"Oh, those kids on the Island were being noisy and woke me right up. I went to check on them."

He must have heard her cry out, too, Geneva thought.

Chapter 13

About 6 a.m., Bob returned to The Blue Gill to find Mike awake, sitting on the cement steps with his head in his hands. The note Bob had left the previous night was in his lap. "Come on in," Bob called out cheerily, "You look like you need coffee." Mike only groaned in response as Bob unlocked the door.

Downing the first cup of coffee that Bob had provided, Mike said, "Thanks. Let me pay you something for your trouble." He patted his pockets then cocked his head to one side as his brow furrowed. "Well, damn." He retraced his steps, going outside to search the area around his car before examining the interior. He came back into the bar. "Bob, it looks like I've lost my wallet."

Bob looked around the stool Mike had occupied the night before. "When was the last time you remember having it?" he asked.

Mike's rueful smile was his only answer. "Right," Bob said, "I'll check the men's room."

Mike continued to look around the bar. With a sigh of relief, he stooped to pick up his wallet from the floor, calling to Bob, "I sort of remember trying to get one last beer off of you last night. I must have dropped it then."

Chapter 14

Weekend mornings were the busiest times of the week at The Yellow Dog. Being located right off the highway, it had gained popularity as a lunch spot for shoppers. Sunday the staff didn't get a break. Folks going to church hit the diner for breakfast early. Those folks that slept in usually started arriving about 9:00 a.m.

Kara welcomed the hectic pace of Sunday morning breakfast. The controlled chaos didn't provide much time for introspection so she was able to go about her various tasks without having to think. Wes barked orders to the cooks, directing the flow of food production with the skill of a conductor directing an orchestra. Kara followed his orders, content to let Wes boss her around.

Blake walked into the diner about 7:30 a.m., stopping Geneva as she walked past him. "Morning, Gennie. Did you see any kids on the island yesterday?"

"Oh, there were a few camping there last night. Why?"

"Well, they got hold of some beer somehow. One of them got scared and rowed to shore early this morning then walked home stinking of alcohol. The rest of the kids' parents showed up shortly after that and took the whole

Chapter 14

bunch home."

Geneva nodded her head. "We did notice some commotion just before sun-up." She knew this would be treated as the next big town scandal. When the talk died down, a new group of kids would do the same thing. "This isn't anything new. Are you letting me in on the gossip to get a free cup of coffee?"

Blake grinned, "Well, a free cup of your coffee, Geneva, is nothing to be taken lightly."

Geneva said, "Flattery, as well?"

Blake smiled. "The thing is, the kids all claim to have heard a gunshot coming from your place early this morning. You know anything about that?"

"No one was shooting while I was at home."

"Well, the kids had been drinking. It could have been anything." He shrugged his shoulders. "I'm guessing a car just backfired; probably Randy's old heap. Well, I had to check it out; part of the job, you know." He grinned flirtatiously as he held out his empty cup.

"Blake, you're such a tease. How can I resist?" She poured him another cup.

"Thanks, Gennie. Let Harold know I'd like to talk to him, too."

"Sure thing," she said.

Harold walked in about 8 a.m. "Is Hollis here? We were going to meet up for breakfast."

Kara said, "Haven't seen him, Pops. By the way, Blake wants to talk with you about the kids on the island last night. They claim to have heard someone shooting a gun."

"Huh? Heard gunshots?" Harold scrunched up his

face. "Sure thing; soon as I meet with Hollis."

Harold hung around the diner for two hours waiting for Hollis to show. Finally, he announced, "Kara, I'm going down to the cabins to see if I can find Hollis. It's strange. He was supposed to meet me here and now he's not even answering his phone."

Harold drove down Lakeshore Road until he came to a police barricade. In short order, he found himself sent back the way he had come.

"The county boys have Lakeshore Road blocked off," Pops explained as he settled down at the counter.

"Well, that explains that. I didn't see the Morrison's or Mrs. Perry this morning. They come up Lakeshore," Geneva replied.

Kara paused. "Must be why I haven't seen Bob this morning. There's no easy way for him to get here with that road blocked. They aren't doing roadwork are they? Sunday isn't usually a day for that."

Harold considered this. "No, they wouldn't have the police blocking the road, or taking over the lodge, for that matter."

Wes had joined them as the breakfast rush dissipated. Sunday lunch-time was usually pretty slow.

Kara agreed with her grandfather. "Nope, I don't think the police would be out in force for roadwork."

Geneva offered, "I've always suspected those upstanding lodge members were a wild bunch. I wouldn't be surprised to find they're running a gambling establishment, with a prostitution ring in the back." The membership of the lodge tended to be middle-aged to older people with the big excitement for the members split between the fall dance, the

Chapter 14

annual holiday raffle, and the spring bake sale.

Kara chuckled at the notion of elderly prostitutes at the old brick federal style building.

"Darn!" Pops scowled, "It's sad to think the town's crime spree has come to an end. Boy, was it a fun ride!" He shook his head, frowning at Geneva. He said, "I am real curious about what's going on. I tried to get into the lodge parking lot, but got run off." He grunted as he got up off the stool. "If Hollis makes it in, let him know he can reach me at home. I'll give Blake a call to see what he wants."

The few lunch-time customers were all speculating about the reason the police had the road shut down. Geneva delivered an order to one of the tables while Kara bused the empty ones.

"Gennie," whispered one of the women at the table, "you must have heard something."

Geneva set the plates of hot food in front of her customers. "Well, Blake was in early this morning. He told me some kids were on the island drinking. I can't imagine they would shut off the road for that. I mean, why would they bring in the state police for kids who are misbehaving? They've been going to that island to drink beer for generations. It must be something else."

The women shook their heads sadly. "Maybe one of the children drowned. It's bound to happen sometime. Do you know whose children they were? Oh, that poor mother!"

As always, the jump from the facts to unwarranted conclusions happened faster than the speed of light. The rumor would be flying around that some child had drowned within the hour. Kara, who had overheard the interchange between the women and her mother, could just picture the flow of old ladies who would be making their way down to the Lodge to catch a glimpse of anything gossip-worthy.

Normally, Kara would keep listening to glean any tidbit of intriguing speculation that might be true, but today she just felt tired and wanted a nap. She realized she was becoming short-tempered as she cleared the tables. When she was able, she retreated to the kitchen where she started washing up dishes.

It was soothing to rinse the dishes before placing them in the dishwasher. Kara watched the warm water stream onto the plates, carrying her anger with it as it ran down the drain. Wes had let most of the kitchen help go home and was busy completing the orders from the lunch stragglers. For a moment, Kara was able to stand alone, engulfed in the steam rising from the dishwasher. She didn't want to think about drowned children or grieving mothers. She recalled how the chaplain at the hospital had urged her to focus on life. Sometimes the faces of the dead were all that crowded her mind. The cries of the dying had filled her dreams for too long. The water swirled down the drain and she forced herself to send these grave thoughts with it.

Wes watched her. He didn't need to understand the demons she had been fighting since she'd returned home. It was enough that he recognized Kara's scars were much more than physical. Geneva had told him one of the survivors had said Kara had been "resolute" as she had protected them. Looking at her now, Wes decided resolute was the word that fit her best. He was well-aware of Kara's temper and knew she had channeled it into saving those lives. Now she carried her memories in silence. He knew those memories

Chapter 14

continued to burned her even more than the hot blast of fuel that had given her the scars she hid from view.

Wes mixed some chocolate milkshakes then walked up to Kara, reaching across her to shut off the water.

"Kara, you look a little warm. How about a double-chocolate milkshake?" He wiggled his eyebrows at her. "After all, chocolate is the key to happiness."

"Am I that obvious? Sorry. It's been a lousy couple of days."

"You do look kind of sad and disheveled. You're all sweaty and sticky."

Souvenirs

Chapter 15

Because the diner was a local hub for information, almost everyone in town was there at least once a week. Of course, the hot topic was the murder. The citizens of Monroe speculated on motives and spent a lot of time debating on methods of murder. The neighborhood watch gained a new focus. Almost immediately, reporters invaded the area, and of course, the police seemed to be everywhere.

Monroe had gone so long without much notice by the surrounding world that the sudden attention was a little dazzling. Evening news reporters vied for the best location to use as a backdrop. Newspaper articles were covering everything from the history of Monroe to Hollis Meyers's life. There was no shortage of on-the-street interviews with locals. It didn't seem to matter that most of the locals interviewed didn't even know Hollis had existed, let alone that he was in Monroe. Within 48 hours, everyone seemed to be an expert. There was no limit to speculation or outlandish theories for the motive.

The only ones not talking, it seemed, were the Dyers.

"Gennie, I haven't seen Harold for a day or two. Is he okay?" Bob asked gently one afternoon.

"Harold's fine. He's been burning up the phone lines

Chapter 15

and driving over to Lafayette to talk with some professor friends of his."

"He's driving all the way to Purdue? What's that old goat up to?"

"I'm not real certain. I think it has something to do with Hollis. Pops has been carrying around those blueprints everywhere he goes." Gennie patted Bob's arm. "I'll have him give you a call when I see him next."

Kara was circling with the coffee pot. The elderly women at the table leaned forward in anticipation, wide-eyed as they waited their turn to one-up the other's information.

"I heard he was one of those nasty drug dealers from Los Angeles. He was trying to set up shop at the school."

"No, he was stalking his ex-wife. Her new boyfriend shot him out of jealousy."

Kara barely suppressed a smile. She moved closer to the table. "Kara, you had dealings with that awful man."

"What man?" She replied innocently.

The old woman closest to her swatted at Kara. "Stop teasing! That man from the West Coast who made Harold so angry. Was he a drug dealer?"

"I wouldn't say I knew Mr. Meyers all that well, although I did make his acquaintance."

"I thought you had words with him."

"Yeah, we had a disagreement, but Mr. Meyers seemed to be a nice man. His ex-wife took a job in Fort Wayne and he wanted to be close to his daughters. That's why he relocated from Washington state. He wanted to be close to his girls," Kara said.

The trio of elderly women looked disappointed.

Souvenirs

"More coffee?" Kara's changing the subject drew icy stares. The women once again huddled over the table as they tried with all their might to keep the gossip going.

Kara walked into the kitchen. "They're buzzing out there today," Wes acknowledged.

Kara looked back over her shoulder. "It's every kind of wrong, Wes. Everyone has some dark secret. I don't think Hollis is any different, but I don't see why anyone would want to kill him." Her eyes darkened. "I liked him and I'm real sorry he's gone." Kara locked eyes with Wes. "I'm really upset someone here in Monroe killed him."

She waved her hand toward the dining room. "Look at them! They're either forming into neighborhood watch groups or doing the conspiracy theory stuff," she shook her head. "Reporters are everywhere. Folks who are usually sensible are making fools of themselves to get their face on-camera." She placed her hands on her hips. "What they need to do is stay out of the way of the police. People have started to point fingers at their neighbors. Why would anyone here want to kill a newcomer to the community?"

"Kara, people are people. Monroe is only a wide place in the road. This is the most exciting thing to happen here since one of your ancestors found his way to the lake and set the local Wea tribe atwitter."

"They'll find the killer; everyone will be all surprised then the conversation on the motive will take over." Wes tossed an apron to Kara. "In a few months, life will return to normal. To promote that normalcy, how 'bout you peel some potatoes?"

Kara snatched the apron out of the air. "I'm sorry, but I'm really upset over this. I did like Hollis. What's really

Chapter 15

bothering me is that it happened here."

Wes watched Kara change before his eyes, her demeanor darkening. In a flash, she wasn't the damaged girl who came home from the war.

"Heaven help the murderer," he thought.

Chapter 16

Snatching up the mouse, Stan started searching through online real estate listings. Something flashed past that caught his eye. His hand paused over the mouse. He opened another site. Leaning forward he clicked his mouse to opened another page. He threw himself back in his chair laughing. He hit the print button. "Well, I'll be," he whispered.

Impatient, he jerked the document from the printer and examined it. The smile spread slowly over his face into a full blown smirk. He nodded his head. "Fortune is smiling on me today. One door closes another opens." He thumped the piece of paper. "This will be the deal that will allow me to move out of this stinking town. I don't need you Mr. Hollis Meyers. You may have cut me out, but the joke is on you because it doesn't matter. There's bigger fish in this pond." Stan laughed at his own joke.

Stan walked back to the diner before lunch service ended. Looking around the dining room he swaggered over to the counter seating. Greeting diners as he passed them, he sat down smiling at Kara.

"What?"

"I'm smiling. It's still okay to smile isn't it?"

Chapter 16

"Sure. I like a smiling face. You know what you want?"

"I believe I do know what I want." He continued looking at Kara. "I think I might even know how to get it."

Kara pulled the order pad from her apron, tapping it with the pencil.

"Oh, you mean food. I'll take a BLT, onion rings and a cherry coke. You know the kind with the cherry at the bottom. Like a hidden gem that only takes a little bit of work to get to," he winked.

Kara was on full alert. Growing up she had learned that he was always cocky when he could smell money. Her eyes darkened. Stan was smelling money.

Kara said, "Is that all?"

"Are we still talking about food?"

She placed the order with Wes. While she made Stan's cherry coke she watched him sitting at the counter in animated conversation with some of the regulars. Pleased with himself today, Stan was almost giddy in sharp contrast to his prior performance.

"Here you go. Cherry on the bottom like you asked for."

Stan said, "The last time we talked I thought you were going to hit me."

Kara flashed him a smile. "Oh, Stan, when was the last time I hit you? It must be years ago. I've grown past that now."

One of the old guys coughed.

Stan said, "Sophomore year in high school."

"See years ago. I don't do that anymore."

Another cough sounded from down the counter.

Souvenirs

Kara turned to smile in the direction of the sound. Several diners seemed to be looking for portents in the bottom of their coffee mugs.

Kara turned back to Stan. "So what have you been up to? Making any sales?"

"No. Can't say the real estate business has been hugely profitable in this area. Hollis' project was pretty good. That would have been a terrific deal for me. Might still be. I believe his wife is working in Chicago."

You little bottom feeder, Kara thought. Kara forced herself to continue smiling. Leaning in she nodded her head. "You didn't look so confident when you left last time. You look right chipper now."

"Do I? I feel chipper. On top of the world."

Kara's Stan radar was humming. Something unethical was going on. Stan was going to end up burning himself along with anyone standing next to him. "Got a new deal going?"

"My goodness, you are the little conversationalist. Last time we talked you weren't as friendly."

I wouldn't be speaking to you now you little weasel if you weren't up to something, Kara thought. "Well, it sounded to me like you were not anywhere close to happy that Pops was talking to Hollis without you. Sounded to me like you were a bit worried."

Stan's face got serious. "Hollis thought he could use me. He thought I was some convenient hick he could cut out once the contacts are made." Stan cleared his throat. "Not to speak ill of the dead," he mumbled. Taking a nastier tone he hissed, "That little scheme didn't work out so well, did it?"

Chapter 16

Kara turned to grab napkins in order to calm herself just as Stan's order came up. "Stan, you should know Hollis defended you to Pops."

"Defending me, huh? Well, at least the man knew quality when he saw it." Stan reached out to pat her hand. Kara could feel the tidal wave of her anger rising. She noticed Walt, one of Pops cronies, sitting at the end of the counter watching her. He glanced at the guy sitting beside him then both men turned to glare at Stan.

Kara thought, Okay. Calm down. If you scare off Stan, you won't find out what he's up to. She attempted to relax her shoulders. If he messes with Pops again, I'm going to pound him.

Noticing his empty glass, she asked Stan, "Do you need a refill? I'll give you one for free." She gave him her best customer-service smile. "I'll even throw in a new cherry."

"Well, aren't you sweet?" Stan pushed his glass at her.

Setting the refill down in front of Stan, Kara asked, "So, what do you have cooking?"

"Not a thing. Simply waiting for the right moment. Timing is everything."

"Big sale?"

"Not yet. I'm looking at getting in on the ground floor of something to provide a more long-term cash flow. You know, I've got to think about my future. It'll take a careful hand to land this fish." He took a bite from his sandwich. "A very careful hand."

Kara raised her eyebrows, thinking, The little weasel isn't going to tell me.

Souvenirs

"Ah", she commented, "Have the brass ring in your sights"

She stood there for a bit to see if he would say anything else, but he just winked at her, making her furious. She fought to hold her anger in check, wiping down the counter in an effort to remain calm. Stan called after her, "I guess only realtors check listings. The internet is a marvelous thing!"

She thought, You baboon! Why would I check real estate listings? He must be doing something sneaky with property. Attempting to find out more, she turned back to him. "You're doing pretty well then?"

Stan retorted, "Think I'll get me one of those exotic sports cars. What color would you choose?"

"How about pink?"

Stan burst out laughing and Kara observed Walt giving her a curious glance. At this point, she decided she was wasting her time talking to Stan, yet she thought, He better not be pulling anything that involves the family. She sent a fake smile his way before going back to the dining room.

Suddenly, Kara saw Stan jump up, leaving three fives on the counter before rushing outside. Geneva, surprised, picked up the bills. She had never known Stan to leave a tip of any kind, let alone over-pay.

Once he returned to his office, Stan stamped the Hollis Meyers file closed then tossed it into his file basket. He started another on-line search through high-end real estate listings. "I wonder why –" he muttered to himself. The flash of color that had caught his eye in the diner flashed past again. He glanced out the window at the passing traffic.

Chapter 16

Eyes alight with greed; he snatched a blank contract from the drawer and rushed out, slamming the door behind him.

Geneva stuck her head into the kitchen. "Has anyone seen Harold? He's been spending all his time on the farm poking around."

"Nope. He said he was trying to avoid the reporters, but he put it in more colorful terms than I just did," Wes said.

Geneva rolled her eyes. "Stubborn old coot! I'm going to have to start making breakfast and lunch for him before I leave."

Souvenirs

Chapter 17

On Tuesday afternoon Kara and Geneva were preparing dinner when there was a soft knock on the kitchen door. "What a pleasant surprise! I can't remember the last time you had a meal with us. Come on in! Can you stay for dinner?" Geneva wiped her hands on a towel and opened the screen door.

Kara turned from peeling carrots to smile at their visitor. "Hey, Blake!"

He didn't return the women's smiles as he took off his hat. "Is Harold in? I saw his truck out front."

Geneva suddenly looked concerned. "What's going on?" Kara stopped peeling carrots and noticed the air seemed to thicken. She turned to face Blake.

"Geneva, I'm here on official business. Can I talk to Harold?"

"Kara, go get your grandfather."

She found him pouring over some paperwork in the living room. "Pops, Blake is here to see you. He says it's official."

Harold looked up at Kara. "Well, I wonder what that could be about." He followed her back to the kitchen.

"What do you need Blake?"

Chapter 17

"Can I have that old gun of yours? The one you keep in the case in the living room?"

"Why?"

"Harold, I can get a search warrant, but I'd rather we do it this way."

"Why?" This time Harold was louder. Kara moved closer to her grandfather.

Blake's steady gaze didn't waiver from Harold's face. He continued, "Harold, I need to look at that war trophy of yours. You carried it home from Korea, right? It's unique in that it fires a hard-to-come by bullet. The bullet they pulled out of Mr. Meyers is one of those special bullets. You have a Nagant M1895 revolver don't you?"

Harold grabbed the back of the chair. "I don't even own any bullets to that gun. I've never even fired it. I don't remember the last time I had it out of the case." Harold was leaning on the chair with a bewildered look on his face. Kara moved behind him to steady him, breathing heavily with her mind racing. The gun. Something was tickling at the edges of her awareness. What about that gun?

Blake said levelly, "Then that will be what we find and you don't have anything to worry about." Kara recognized the authority in his tone and her chest tightened.

Geneva was looking from Blake to Harold. "Pops, give him the gun. Blake is doing us a favor. It isn't going to do any harm to let him have it."

While Kara helped her grandfather sit down in a chair at the table, Geneva said, "Kara, get Pops some lemonade. Blake, come with me." Blake's professional demeanor fell for a second. He shot a guilty glance at Harold and confronted Kara's burning glare.

Souvenirs

Turning back to her grandfather, she squatted on the floor beside him. "Pops, you okay?"

"I'm okay, Little Bit. I'm okay." His mind was someplace else as he stared out the back door. Kara was confused; she didn't understand her grandfather's reaction. The gun had been in its case forever. There weren't any rounds for it in the house and those bullets weren't something you picked up at the local store. The last time Kara remembered that old gun being out was while she was still in high school. It had been years ago when Pops last oiled it. To her knowledge he had never used it. It was just something he had brought back from Korea with him, a souvenir. It was the only thing he brought back, unless you counted Bob.

"Pops, you don't look so good."

Harold dropped his head and rubbed the bridge of his nose.

Kara went to the fridge to get him some lemonade. When she turned back around she was stunned by how old he looked. He was well into his seventies, but she had never thought of him as old. He had always radiated so much energy, but in a matter of minutes, he had aged before her eyes. The light had gone out of him. As he cradled his head in his hands, his elbows on the table, he actually looked defeated. Her chest tightened with panic for him. Pops!, she thought desperately, Why are you acting like this? I don't understand!

Hearing Blake's footsteps, she turned to find him holding a plastic bag with the gun in it. Geneva followed him into the kitchen, stunned to see Harold slumped over the table. She put her hand on Blake's arm, steering him firmly to the door. After making a visual assessment of Harold, she went to the phone. Harold was unaware of her activities or the lemonade sitting in front of him. He just sat there, unmoving.

Doc Marr burst in the front door without knocking. "Harold, what are you doing?" Harold didn't respond, his face a mask as he stared out the screen door. "Harold, look at me!" Doc Marr grabbed Harold's face, peering into his eyes. "Kara, hand me my bag."

Doc checked Harold's vitals before looking up at Geneva. "Gennie, an ambulance should be getting here in a few minutes. Good thing I was buying honey down at the co-op, so I was close. For Pete's sake, Harold, look at me!"

The doctor examined him. "Kara, go make sure the ambulance doesn't miss your driveway. All those trees hide it."

Harold didn't say a word, didn't look at anyone, and didn't respond. Doc Marr cursed. Harold remained unresponsive as he was situated onto the gurney. "Gennie, we're going to find out what's going on with him."

Kara was numb. She didn't remember getting her mom into the car or driving to the hospital. Stiff-legged, she somehow made her way to the emergency room through the looming doors and sat in the waiting room, feeling disconnected and absent as she drank hot cocoa that tasted like coffee from the vending machine. Snatching a journal from the pile on the plastic table, she stared at the same advertisement for a long while. The sounds of the hospital only added to the waves of nausea sweeping over her.

"Where is he? Gennie, where is he? Kara, what happened?" Bob rushed over to them. "What happened?"

Souvenirs

The older woman at the desk glared at Bob and he gave her an apologetic look.

"Oh, sorry, sorry!" He looked at Kara. "Sorry."

Geneva gave Bob a hug. Harold often joked that the reason Bob had stayed in Monroe was because his parents had fed a stray. "Once you do that you can't get rid of them," he would say. The two had been close friends through the years. Kara realized this must be difficult for Bob as well, but his presence felt invasive. She slipped down into her seat, hiding her displeasure with him behind the magazine, while trying to block the soft murmurs of explanation and comfort her mother offered Bob.

"Blake did what? Where is Harold? I've got to talk to him. Now!" Bob's head swiveled.

Kara was stunned. Bob's response was not quite what she had anticipated. Something wasn't right. It dawned on her Pops might be a suspect in the murder because of that gun. What was it about a gun?, she demanded of herself. Pops had been acting strange the past couple days and Pops' behavior when Blake had taken the gun frightened Kara. Now Bob was acting odd as well. Although Kara's thoughts were scattered in a million different directions, a small part of her mind was seeing the situation clearly. She was aware something was out of place. There were thoughts chipping away at the panic, trying to surface, trying to make her realize something.

Kara closed her eyes. Fear wouldn't do anyone any good. She studied Bob, who looked flushed and ready to have a heart attack. Her focus then turned to her mother who was attempting to calm him, her face etched with worry. How does she stay so calm? Kara wondered. Kara

Chapter 17

knew she needed do the same thing. Letting her emotions rule her now would not help Pops. *Why can't I see what's wrong here?* she thought, her head hurting. She couldn't deal with Bob right now.

She told her mom she was going for a walk. She worked to clear her head as she sat outside on a bench watching people coming in and out of the hospital. She wandered around to the emergency entrance where she sat on the curb, watching pigeons hop in the driveway looking for handouts.

"Don't feed them or they won't ever leave you alone," Wes commented as he approached. "How's Harold doing?"

His words were glib, as usual, but his face was full of concern. He sat on the curb next to Kara. "So, what I hear is the police came to arrest Harold for murdering that guy then Harold had a nervous breakdown. How far off is the rumor?"

"Blake took the gun Pops brought back from Korea. He didn't come to arrest him." She leaned against Wes. "I don't know what's wrong with Pops."

He put his arm around her. "I see." They watched the pigeons. "If you think you'll be okay out here I'll go find your mom. Or better yet, why don't we go in together? You can show me where the old codger is," Wes suggested.

Kara spotted Bob, who was pacing in the waiting room, but Geneva was nowhere in sight. His words came in a torrent. "The doctor took Gennie to Harold's room, but they won't let me go in." His eyes were filled with tears. "I don't know where I would be if it weren't for Harold! When the war was over, I didn't have anyone. There was no place to go home to. He brought me here and his parents said I could stay as long as I wanted. He was my best man when I married Gail. I stood up with him when he married your grandmother. Harold's parents even loaned me the money to buy The Blue Gill from Old Man Morrison. I don't know what I would do if anything happened to him!"

Kara's anger drained out of her as she listened. This man standing in front of her would do anything for Pops, but like her, he was unable to do a blessed thing right now. She put her arms around him, understanding how he felt.

Wes rose to embrace Geneva as she walked over to him. Pushing away gently, Geneva turned to Kara. "Pops is okay. Doc Marr said he's a strong old coot and gave him a sedative. He may be in shock. For the most part the news is good. Doc says his heart is just fine. He didn't have a stroke, but they're going to keep him for observation. They want to see the test results to be sure he's okay." Drained, Geneva sank into one of the chairs.

"Thank God!" was all Bob could say.

Geneva suggested, "I'm going to take the first shift. Kara, you can spell me in the morning." She held up her hand as her daughter protested. "Go get some sleep. Wes, please take Kara and Bob home." Wes saluted. Geneva cut Bob off before he could say anything. "Now Bob, you're not in any shape to drive so let Wes take you home. You can come back tomorrow morning to get your car. Same for you Kara."

After dropping Bob off at his house, Wes stopped by The Yellow Dog to put a "closed until Thursday" sign on the door.

"I'm going to pick up a few things at my place," Wes said.

Chapter 17

He insisted on staying the night at the house with Kara, sleeping on the couch in the living room. Before they called it a night, he made phone calls to the diner's staff.

"Kara, I made you some soup." he said. She ate mechanically without tasting, knowing full well she wouldn't be able to sleep.

Souvenirs

Chapter 18

"Kara, you ever going to wake up? Breakfast is on the table!" Wes shouted from the kitchen.

When Kara came downstairs, she found an amazing breakfast waiting for her. Wes certainly can cook, she thought. The sun was well up in the sky over the tree tops when they left for the hospital.

When Wes and Kara arrived at the hospital, Bob was already there. Geneva said that the nurse reported Harold had slept well. Doc Mar was expected to stop by later that morning. Geneva allowed Wes to lead her out to the car and drive her home.

Bob and Kara were able to get in to see her grandfather when they arrived at the hospital later in the morning.

"Little Bit, can I talk to Bob alone for a few minutes?"

Kara was concerned by this request. She left the room spending the time wandering around the waiting room and flipping through stacks of outdated magazines until Bob walked right past her. Puzzled, Kara tilted her head to one side as he headed for the door without even making eye contact. She followed him, waiting while he made a phone call from the payphone in the lobby.

"Bob, you okay?" she asked gently.

Bob jerked around. "Kara, look, I called my oldest son to let him know I'd be at the bar later. I have things I need to do. You probably should spend time with your grandfather."

Kara's eyes grew wide at his dejected tone. His expression was distant and downcast. "Bob, what's wrong? What did Pops say to you?"

"Child, you need to talk to your grandfather." He turned abruptly and walked out the door.

Kara watched Bob walk away. Sounds that had gone unnoticed suddenly sharpened. She could hear the nurses softly talking, the intercom announcements and unseen machinery humming. Swallowing became difficult. Her chest tightened. She studied Bob as he shuffled through the parking lot before she turned down the hall toward Harold's room.

Glancing back to Bob, her eyes narrowed. What's going on? Kara spun around sharply, barely missing a collision with someone carrying flowers. Murmuring an apology, she stalked back to her grandfather's room.

"Is Bob okay?" she demanded. "He called his son to let him know he's going to be late to work."

Harold cocked a bushy eyebrow. "Well, he's got a life outside of his business to take care of."

"He seems really upset. I know he's mad at Blake; so am I. You scared all of us!" Kara pulled at the blankets on the bed. "There's something else going on. What did you say to Bob?"

Harold bowed his head, rubbing his eyes. "Don't be

mad at Blake. He's doing the job we pay him to do." Harold lay back on the pillows, closing his eyes.

Kara's throat tightened. He looked so old, so frail. Her tone softened. "Pops, I asked you, what's going on?"

He grimaced. "Doc Marr says I'm a faker. He said he should charge me triple for wasting his time." In spite of herself, a soft smile played around Kara's eyes.

"Kara," he motioned her to come over to him. "Little Bit, if something should happen --"

Kara said, "Pops, nothing is going to happen."

He took her hand. "Kara, if something should happen to me, you're a Dyer. Your mom is one of the best people I know. She isn't a Dyer though. A Dyer has always taken care of the lake. We always have."

Kara frowned. "Of course, I'll take care of the lake. You know I will. Harry is a Dyer, too."

Harold patted her hand. "Yes, Harry is a Dyer. He's a doctor; his interests are elsewhere. You love the lake. You were going to school to become an ecologist. You know the lake in ways he doesn't. You have the desire to protect it. You need to be strong to protect the lake. I'm getting too old."

She didn't know what to say. She wasn't strong. She didn't want to be responsible for anything. Pops wasn't old. No, not Pops. She was having difficulty breathing and couldn't get air into her lungs. She touched the scar where the shrapnel had torn open her side as she felt the panic rise up again. She tried to understand what he meant by "if something should happen". The room was spinning. She sat down in the chair near the bed, still regarding her grandfather with incomprehension. "But Doctor Marr said

Chapter 18

you're okay."

Before Harold could reply, a nurse came into the room. Without looking at Kara she checked Harold's vitals. Kara stood in the far right corner away from the monitors. Frowning, she listened to the nurse talk softly to Harold. She placed her hand on the chair to steady herself, still wondering what was going on as she stared at the cartoon animals on the nurse's smock.

Thoughts raced through her mind. What made Pops act the way he did? Something here isn't right. The gun, he freaked out about that old gun. Why? Kara's skin paled as her knees buckled. She slid into the chair. Could he have killed Hollis? What would be the reason? Her mind reeled with these questions as the nurse went through her examination. Pops isn't telling me something. Why? What could it be that he doesn't want me to know? When the nurse left the room Kara was shaking. She cleared her throat. "Pops, something isn't right here. What's going on? Why are you so worried about the gun?"

Harold watched her flashing eyes and saw the resolution in her posture. "Little Bit, I saw we could make money by developing the land in the manner Hollis proposed. I got greedy, that's all. I was going to move forward with his proposal without him. I talked to people who knew about these things. We would make a neat little profit without harming the lake. Hollis found out and got mad. I felt like I needed to protect myself, so I got out that old gun. We got into a fight. Yes, I shot him."

The room started spinning. Moving quickly to a battle-ready stance, she sent the chair she had been sitting in crashing into the wall behind her. Momentarily speechless, she stood with her mouth hanging open, shaking her head in disbelief. Her voice finally returning, she shouted, "When have you ever cared about a profit from the lake?"

"Kara, calm down! I've already called Blake. He should be here any minute."

She spun toward the door, stopping to grip the edge of the chair so tight she broke a fingernail. She was too stunned to move and her head felt like it was about to explode. Between clenched teeth she said, "Mom – does Mom know?"

"No."

She spun to face him. "Pops, you couldn't have. You wouldn't have. That isn't like you."

"Little Bit, I did."

Kara grabbed the chair, flinging it into the hall, her eyes dark, angry pools. Blake wasn't going to take him away. He would have to get past her first. The late morning light coming through the window caught her auburn hair, her hands unclenched, ready to move. "No," she whispered. "No!" she shouted. The sound echoed down the halls, causing the nurses to rush into the room. "No!" she yelled again. Anxious eyes watched Kara as they checked on Harold. Other nurses came into the room, placing themselves between Kara and her grandfather. Kara shoved them aside like so much fluff.

"Kara, stop!" Harold's voice resounded over all the commotion. "You aren't doing anyone any good by acting like that! Sit down!" He sat up in bed as she turned to him. Now he looked like the Pops she knew, not like some weak, defeated old man.

Chapter 18

"Get out!" he ordered the nurses, "Out!" Kara stood almost at attention, staring at her grandfather. Her eyes were still smoldering when Doc Marr ran in with Blake.

"Harold, what in the name of Sam Hill do you think you're doing? I don't believe this for a minute!" Doc Marr turned to Kara. "Young lady, behave yourself! Kara Dyer, I slapped your behind when you were born. I won't permit you to scare these nurses. What would your mother think? You come with me, young lady!"

His harsh words were not reflected in the kind eyes under enormous white eyebrows.

The wrath that had taken hold of Kara slowly drained away. She took a deep breath. She felt totally disconnected as she took the arm Doc Marr offered to her. She allowed herself to be led from the room.

"Thanks, Doc," Harold called after them.

Doc Marr glared at Kara, saying again, "Come with me, young lady." He seated her in the waiting room then pulled a light from his pocket, flashing it in her eyes. "Well, you're in a state. I'm giving you a sedative."

Kara shook her head. "No, I'm fine."

Doc Marr tilted her head back. "No, you aren't. You're shaking." He checked her pulse. Turning to the nurse's station he shouted, "Let's get a blanket over here," he said. "Bring some juice."

"No sedative, Doc," she murmured.

Everything seemed surreal. The air seemed thick and it took so long to move. Her head pounding, she looked intently at Doc Marr sitting beside her, trying to understand what he was saying. Someone wrapped a blanket around her as the hard edges of a juice box were pushed into her hand.

Souvenirs

Later, she was aware she walked out to Doc Marr's car.

When they arrived at the house, Kara vaguely wondered about the driveway being full of cars. Someone was holding her elbow. The house seemed to be full of people. It's a nightmare like all the others," she thought frantically. I'm going to wake up soon in a sweat and everything will be okay. Doc Marr sat her on the back porch, pulling the hospital blanket tightly around her before entering the kitchen to talk with Geneva.

Chapter 19

The lake's breeze blew the summer heat away. The sound of the water lapping softly against the dock floated up from the lake, calling to her. Unseeing, she walked stiffly down to the dock toward the soft murmur of whispered comfort. The air was so cool and gentle. She could hear the sound of the locust thrumming in the trees, like a dream. She found herself in the lake, swimming. The water glided past her as she floated, relaxed, clearing her mind.

Kara swam to the island and wandered up the small beach where she examined the vacated camp site. So many times she had sat beside a similar camp site here. She turned to look back at the dock where the house was full of people. The lake shimmered and glistened under the summer sun.

It was late afternoon when she woke up. The cooling air was causing gentle waves to lap up against the shore. She rolled over in the soft sand. A discarded beer can bounced on the edge of the water.

That's right! she thought. The kids had been drinking; their parents found out, and they showed up at dawn to pull their misbehaving children off the island. They're all grounded for life. Kara smiled as her hand moved the sand into curling patterns.

Souvenirs

She walked back into the lake and swam toward Pops' dock. She kept remembering something about a gun. Like the empty beer can caught in the flotsam at the shore, it kept bumping against her memory. A gun. A gun shot. The kids claimed to have heard gun shots in the predawn morning. They had claimed it came from the house. Had they been drunk when they claimed to have heard it? Was it a car backfiring like Blake said it was? Damn Blake! Why would there be a gun shot from here when the murder took place across the lake?

She reached out with each stroke, stretching, moving forward. Pops got home around 1 a.m. Sunday morning. Kara had been awakened by the unique sound of the ancient truck's old engine and had checked the clock when she heard the truck pull into the driveway. She was awake again at 3:30 p.m. because of the nightmare, which was about the time the murder had occurred, according to the local gossip. Kara realized Pops walked in the back door about the same time, wearing his nightshirt. She started treading water. She looked toward the side of the Lake where the Indian Rest Cabins were. Her mind snapped to attention. Pops couldn't have committed the murder! He was on this side of the lake. He couldn't have killed Hollis then rowed back from Indian Rest Cabins in time to walk in the back door at 3:35 p.m. She would've heard the motor boat or the truck. The timeline didn't work. Pops couldn't have done it! But why did he say he had?

She continued toward the dock, gliding through the water. Her mind sharpened. Why was her grandfather lying? Why is the gun important? Her memory of what happened that night flickered. She couldn't figure it all out,

Chapter 19

but it really didn't matter because she knew Pops hadn't killed anyone.

Floating in the lake just a few yards beyond the dock, she suddenly heard someone shout, "Gennie, she's over here!" Kara returned to treading water.

"Kara, what are you doing? We've been looking all over for you!" Doc Marr was on the dock with his hands on his hips, looking like thunder.

"I'm swimming. Care to join me?"

Doc Marr looked stern. "You must still be in shock. Come inside. You're worrying your mother."

Kara splashed water at him.

"Hey, stop fooling around and give me your hand. People are worried about you and here you are, floating around in the lake." Geneva ran down the dock towards her and Kara shouted, "Mom, Pops didn't kill Mr. Meyers! He couldn't have!"

Geneva paused, glanced over at Doc Marr. "Blake called. He said that old gun hadn't been fired. How did you know?"

"Think about it. We were up between 3:15 a.m. and 3:30 a.m. that morning, which is about the time the gossip chain claims the murder happened. Pops couldn't have rowed over to the other side of the lake in the dark, shot Hollis then rowed back to come busting in the door by 3:35 a.m. If he'd taken the motor boat, we would've heard it. He was with us the rest of the morning until I left for the diner."

Geneva frowned. "You're right. He couldn't have rowed over there in that time." She plopped down in a deck chair. "I'm positive I didn't hear any outboard motor going."

Doc Marr said, "I can confirm the murder happened

sometime between 3:10 a.m and 5 a.m. The neighbor didn't find the body until about 8 a.m. Blake told me that Meyers made a call to Seattle at 2:50 a.m. which was twenty minutes long. He was still alive at 3:10 a.m."

Grinning Kara pulled herself up on the dock. "See?" Kara exclaimed. "He couldn't have done it! When we left for the diner, it was starting to get light. People were waking up and would have heard the gun shot. Those kids' parents were all over the island by then." Her dark eyes flashing, Kara continued, "Mom, at 3:35 a.m. Pops was sitting in the kitchen drinking tea with us."

Geneva said, "I don't understand why he confessed to something he didn't do."

"I don't know either, Mom, but I'm going to find out."

Doc Marr grunted, "I think I'll order an enema for Harold."

Kara left Blake a message then spent the rest of the afternoon gently escorting the remaining "guests" out of the house. She talked her mother into letting her re-open the diner the next day.

The past two days had been a real roller coaster for Geneva. Harold wasn't the only one she'd been worried about. Today, as she watched Kara directing traffic and issuing orders, she was pleasantly surprised. Her daughter hadn't shown this much interest in anything since returning home from Germany.

When the last guest had gone Kara turned to her mother. "It's unfortunate Pops confessed before they found out about the gun. If he had told the truth, he wouldn't be in jail now. Let's go visit the old coot."

Chapter 20

Harold grinned at Kara. "So, you managed to come see me in my distress."

Kara grabbed his hand across the table. "Pops, we figured out you didn't have time to kill Hollis then get back to the house by 3:30 a.m. Besides, Blake said your gun wasn't fired."

Harold's head dropped.

Geneva said, "You didn't kill Hollis, did you?"

Harold's head remained down, unwilling to look his family in the eye.

"Pops, why are you confessing to something you didn't do? None of this makes any sense to me," Kara said.

Harold raised his head. "It doesn't matter, Little Bit."

Geneva hit the table with her fist. "Someone killed Hollis. As long as you sit here holding to this lie, you're letting the real killer go free."

Harold's eyes were fixed on the table. "You figured all this out, Little Bit?"

She nodded.

Harold whispered, "Well, well."

Geneva demanded, "Pops, you need to tell the truth."

Souvenirs

Harold continued to look at the table.

Kara's eyes darkened. "Does the person you're protecting want you to lie for them?"

Harold sat silently.

"You couldn't have done it. I think you know who did. For some strange reason, you're trying to take the fall. Do you think Mom would murder someone? Or maybe you think it's Harry gone mad with too much stress from med school? Or me? So you think I went all PTS and killed off Hollis? Or is one of your cronies actually a killer on the loose?"

Harold shifted uneasily.

"Pops, what are you thinking? You should be helping find the murderer. Playing the stubborn old man is only letting a killer get away!"

"I see." He looked at the sleeve of his jail coveralls. He turned to the guard. "Could you please excuse us so my family can give me the saw?"

The guard raised an eyebrow.

Geneva said, "Pops, you put your foot in it this time. Even if we can convince the police you're innocent, you lied to them. In spite of the fact you think it's for a good reason, you're not helping anyone."

Harold turned back again to the guard. "See, they're even harder on me than you are. It's safe to let me go. I'll be punished for this for years."

The guard raised the other eyebrow.

Harold turned back to Kara. "Kara, you hold the guard, and I'll steal his keys while Geneva keeps a look-out."

Geneva scowled.

The guard shook his head.

Chapter 20

"This is serious, and joking about it won't make it go away! Furthermore, lying about it does more than impede the investigation; it creates heartache for the rest of us," Geneva scolded.

Harold bit his lip. Looking down he pulled on his ear. "I reckon you'd better go now."

Chapter 21

Kara and Geneva arrived at the diner before the sun came up and had the grill going before Wes got in.

"So, I'm no longer necessary, eh? Trying to get me fired?" Wes stood with his hands on his hips, eyes slit.

Geneva elbowed him. "Oh, sorry, Wes. I didn't see you standing there all in the way and everything."

"Well, excuse me for trying to work," he sulked.

"Now, Wes, why would I fire you? You're the one man I can shout orders at and have you obey my slightest whim," Geneva teased.

"I think I'm being harassed." Wes's face changed from a wry grin to a more serious look as he regarded Geneva. Moving toward her, he asked gently, "How's Harold?"

Geneva turned slightly toward the dining room. "He's as well as can be expected. He's an old man who confessed to murdering someone he just met. He's in jail."

Wes put his arm around her, pulling her into him. "Harold is a tough old bird, and he certainly didn't murder anyone."

Kara walked into the kitchen in time to witness the embrace. Her mouth dropped open. She barked, "He

Chapter 21

couldn't have done it! The timeline just doesn't work!"

"What?" Wes's bald head wrinkled as he released Geneva.

Both Kara and her mom blushed.

Kara continued speaking a little too fast to cover her embarrassment. "He couldn't have rowed back from Indian Rest in time to be standing in our kitchen at 3:30 a.m. Not possible. Mom and I had eyes on him from then until a little before 5 a.m."

Wes looked first at Geneva, then at Kara. "Then why is he saying he did it?"

"That's the real question, isn't it?" Geneva pondered.

"No, the big question is, who is he protecting? I suppose having him in jail right now isn't a bad idea either. The real killer thinks he's safe, thanks to that stupid confession. With Pops in jail, nobody's paying attention to the one who did it. This lie Pops invented isn't the only thing wrong here. Things are off-center somehow. We're missing something. It's like a word on the tip of your tongue that you can't remember; it's almost there." Kara's eyes were distant, trying to think.

Wes looked at Geneva as Kara refocused on her mom. "I'll figure out what it is. I'll find out what Pops knows."

She glanced toward the dining room. "Pretty soon that room out there will be full. I'm convinced Pop's confession and arrest is all over Monroe now. They'll be out there gossiping, which is a good thing. Someone will remember something; maybe even say something to spark my memory."

The usual breakfast customers did start coming,

as well as folks Kara didn't see in the diner that often. She noticed more than a few strangers she pegged as reporters eating at the counter. By 7:45 a.m., Geneva had to call in some of the weekend staff. Conversation was subdued at first as the crowd seemed to be waiting for something. Kara decided to mingle, wanting to see if she could get more buzz going by encouraging the talk.

"Good morning, ladies! It's so nice to see you this morning! How are you all doing?" Kara exclaimed brightly.

The three elderly ladies at the table regarded her with a mixture of greed and curiosity. "You're so sweet, you poor dear. We heard the terrible news about your grandfather. Of course, we don't believe a word of it. All lies! How is he doing?"

"Oh, you know Pops. Ornery as always. He's busy winning the guards over to his side to assist in his jail break," Kara smiled ruefully.

"You poor dear," one of the ladies whispered.

The old ladies tut-tutted in unison, which was exactly what Kara wanted. She continued, "Oh, I'm not worried. You shouldn't be either. I know he couldn't have done it. It's just that he has this old gun he brought back from Korea. It seems the bullets they took from Mr. Meyers' body were from that same type of gun."

"Oh, my! Keeping a gun in the house is only going to get you into trouble. These young men come back from the wars with all kinds of dangerous souvenirs. You didn't bring one of those frightful things back with you, did you?"

Kara continued smiling as she felt the pressure from the holster against her back.

The elderly lady continued. "Always a terrible idea to

have a gun around. So the bullet came from Harold's gun?"

"No, not Pops' gun. The police tested it and it wasn't fired," Kara said frowning. "The bullets came from that type of gun though. The thing is we don't have any of those bullets. I don't even know where to buy them around here."

"That's good to hear, dear. I'm sure your grandfather didn't murder anyone either. The truth will win out. All these policemen we don't know running around making accusations! Our police force is shorthanded now that Forest has gone off to join the Indianapolis squad. If we had a full staff, we wouldn't have all these strange policemen." One of the ladies patted Kara's hand.

"Thank you for saying that." Kara noticed someone at another table signaling to her. "Oh, I've got to go. Thank you again, ladies." She heard the whispers flying from the threesome as she walked away from their table.

Geneva was watching her. Smiling, Kara came back behind the counter. She said, "Kara, what are you up to?"

"Getting the gossip going. That's why business is so good this morning. These people are here to watch the train wreck. They're talking and we'll find out what's going on around town. Someone knows something they don't think is connected. Someone always knows something. The old dears over there will get it started and we can wait to find out what floats to the top."

Geneva narrowed her eyes. "It looks to me like you were the one getting it started."

Kara smiled as she started another pot of coffee.

Stan was in about 9 a.m. He seemed to be in a remarkably good mood; effervescent even. He caught Geneva's eye before swaggering over to her.

Souvenirs

"I heard about Harold. I have to admit it's quite a surprise. You seem to be dealing with it pretty well. Must be a real shock to you."

Geneva bit her tongue. "Neither Kara or I believe he could have committed the murder."

"Really? Well, I'd put my money on that then. Kara, especially, always did have a good head on her shoulders. Even when we were kids she had a good handle on things. Is she around?" He looked over and spotted Kara working the counter. He sat on a stool so she'd be sure to notice him right away.

"Hey, beautiful. Heard you had a date with Mike."

"I did." Kara knew when she went to The Blue Gill everyone would know she'd had a date, but she hadn't factored in Stan's reaction. She'd been putting him off when he had asked her out by telling him she wasn't ready to date yet. It was mostly true. He was aware she had been having difficulty readjusting since returning home. However, as it applied to Stan, it was the truth. She didn't want to go out with Stan, ever.

"Maybe I should give you a call this week. We can go out somewhere more romantic than the local bar."

She tried to smile. The result was something resembling a snarl as her lips peeled away from her teeth. "Right now is not a good time for me with Pops in trouble and all."

Stan looked surprised. "Oh, sorry. I'm a little excited now, that's all. Wasn't thinking. You are ready to start dating though? You went out with Mike, right?"

What could she say? She had gone out with Mike, which opened the door to Stan, at least in his mind. She couldn't believe he didn't know how angry she'd been with him or that he didn't realize her family was in crisis at the moment. How could he think dating was something that was even on her radar now?

"After we get past this thing, I'll think about dating again." She hoped that would put him off for a while. She watched his face. She knew he heard "yes" as his grin widened.

"Great! If you want to talk, I'm here for you."

"Thanks, Stan. I'd better get moving. As you can see, we're pretty busy this morning."

Randy buzzed in about noon for lunch, plopping down at his usual spot at the counter. "Hey, Kara. How you holding up?" he asked.

She patted his arm. He was honestly concerned and she smiled at his worried expression.

"Thanks, Randy. Doing well, considering. It was pretty scary when Pops went into the hospital. Then that stupid confession."

"I heard about that. Someone came into the store this morning saying it was impossible for him to have done it; that the timeline didn't fit. Is that right?"

Kara nodded soberly, keeping her expression neutral. Inwardly she was elated; her plan was working. People were talking.

"That's right. He would have to row back to the house from across the lake in ten or fifteen minutes. He would have been winded at the very least when he walked in the kitchen door. I was awake and didn't hear a motor boat or a car. I didn't even hear him walking up the dock. You know how creaky that thing is. We were with him the entire time after that, drinking tea with our poached eggs."

Randy nodded. "It's nearly two miles across the lake from your dock to Indian Rest. Even at a decent pace it would take a while to row that distance."

Kara nodded her head.

Randy considered, "There's no way he could walk it in that amount of time either. That kid I saw walking up Lakeshore that morning didn't make it home until nearly 5 a.m. I don't think Harold could even drive around the lake that fast in that old rattle trap of his. His truck is almost as pathetic as my car."

Kara had forgotten about the drunk kid who had left the island to walk home. About the time her mother left for the diner they heard the motorboats full of parents coming to take their misbehaving children home in the predawn.

"You run your route down Lakeshore? So you saw Mitch?"

"Didn't know it was Mitch at the time. He was wearing a big black hooded jacket. He didn't turn around when I pulled over to see if he wanted a ride. Didn't know he was drunk or a kid. I would have insisted I take him home if I had. A drunk kid shouldn't be walking around at 4 a.m. in the morning."

"You saw Mitch walking home?" One of the other customers at the counter leaned over to speak to Randy.

"It must have been him. I've been driving that route for a while now. I haven't ever seen anyone out walking at that time of the morning."

Kara walked away, leaving them talking about unusual happenings in the area. She could hear different conversations about the murder and Pops' confession. She hadn't heard anything new yet, but they were talking. At some point something would sift out. Everyone was going to want to put in their two cents. Any specific knowledge they had to add to the story was icing on the cake. Kara was counting on it.

Chapter 22

"Hello, good-looking!" She looked up at the greeting to find Mike sitting at the end of the counter. "How about that free cup of coffee someone promised me?" He winked at her.

She felt a thrill that he was even talking to her and realized she was tingling all over. She hadn't had any contact at all with him since their date. All the concern she had about him not really being interested in her evaporated at the sound of his voice. She realized he'd come into the diner to flirt with her. The possibility of her relationship with Mike growing brought a smile to her lips that she was unable to give to Stan.

She poured his coffee then putting the pot down, walked around the end of the counter to sit next to him.

"Oh, my, don't you have the winning walk. It's not often I get served a good cup of coffee and get my hopes raised at the same time." He lifted her hand to his lips, kissing it as he looked up at her face. "Good to see you again, Starlight." He reached around, brushing the soft strands of her hair back from her face.

Kara's skin was electric.

"You are beautiful." He looked at her with soft

Chapter 22

eyes. "It's gratifying to see I can make you blush, being an Amazon warrior woman and everything. It'll be intriguing to see what making love to an Amazon will be like," he purred. Kara's emotions were humming. He stroked her cheek, running his fingers through her hair again. Kara had to remember to breath. He was seducing her right here in the diner!

Geneva had been busy with the cash register and hadn't noticed the interchange between Mike and her daughter, but Wes had. Watching from the kitchen, he was now standing in front of them at the counter.

"There you are, Kara," he said loudly, making Kara jumped. She hadn't even noticed Wes's approach. Her face was flushed as she glared at him.

Wes bared his teeth in a grin at Mike. "Don't think I know you."

Through clenched teeth, Kara said, "Mike Olson, let me introduce you to our cook, Wes."

Wes glanced at Kara before sticking out a greasy hand to Mike.

Mike stared at the hand Wes was offering. Wes looked surprised. "Oh, guess it's a little greasy from all the cooking." He wiped it off on his apron.

Mike was the only person in the diner all day that hadn't been consumed with curiosity over the murder of Hollis Meyers or Harold's confession. He seemed only to be interested in her and Kara was giddy at the thought. She had started the day encouraging gossip, now Mike had made her forget all about the rumors flying around the diner.

A family stared at her from the table near the counter. Geneva had noticed Wes moving to the counter.

Souvenirs

She walked over and stood near Wes to listen in on the conversation.

Kara said, "Wes, I'm taking my break right now. I'll be back in to help in a second."

Wes didn't move.

Kara ignored Wes and turned to Mike. "Thanks for taking the time to talk with me."

Mike grinned at Wes as he took Kara's hand. "Who wouldn't want to spend time with someone so stunning? Look at you in your cute little apron."

Kara blushed, "You do like creating a stir, don't you? It is nice to have something more fun to focus on."

Mike glanced at Wes again and turned back to Kara. "Sugar, I'm more than happy to focus on you. You seem to be a woman who wants a little excitement."

Wes commented, "Well, right now we're all kind of focused on Harold."

Mike continued to gaze upon Kara and said, "Oh, yeah, sorry. How is the old buzzard doing? Is he in jail?"

"Yes, he is," Wes said.

Irritated, Mike regarded Wes, "So you think he couldn't have done the dirty deed, right?"

Kara bristled somewhat at Mike's tone. "No, I don't just think he couldn't have done it; I know he couldn't have done it. The timeline just doesn't work."

Mike's eye brow went up. "There's a timeline now?"

"Yeah. There was a phone call from Mr. Meyers' cell phone about 2:50 a.m. that lasted about twenty minutes. They think he was killed sometime between 3:30 a.m. and 5 a.m. Pops was standing in the kitchen with Mom and me at 3:35 a.m. He couldn't have done it and gotten back to the house that fast."

Kara felt the heat cooling between them.

"I heard you down there talking to Randy. I guess it would take some pretty hefty rowing to get across the lake that fast and Harold is what, about 80? Regular old fossil, isn't he?"

Kara kept smiling, but she was no longer so pleased Mike was there. The warmness she had felt towards him only moments before had vanished. Mike seemed to withdraw into himself as he shot an angry glance at Wes.

Kara's anger rose as she blamed Wes for the change in Mike's attitude. Mike's gaze had traveled down the counter to Randy and he didn't notice Kara's eyes darkening.

Wes didn't miss it, though. He turned and stalked back to the kitchen.

Still looking at Randy, Mike said, "I don't even think I could row over in ten minutes and I'm a lot younger than old Harold." He looked at Kara, giving her his full attention. "I'm such a dope. You and your family," Mike glanced toward the kitchen, "must be feeling all kinds of hurt. I need to stop being so selfish," he took her hand. "It's just so hard to think of anything else when I'm faced with someone so dazzling."

Kara felt her shoulders relax.

"You really are distracting," he smiled softly. "Really, if there's anything I can do to help, please let me know. I can always woo you and win your family over later."

Chapter 23

Kara hadn't seen Bob come in all day. In fact, she hadn't seen Bob since they'd talked in the hospital. Pops was worried about what Bob had said the last time Kara had spoken with her grandfather. She wanted to find out if Bob knew what Pops was up to. After the diner closed for the day she walked down to Dot's. She had an ice cream cone and waited for The Blue Gill staff to arrive and open the bar.

"Hey, where's Bob?" called Kara. The waitress pointed toward the back of the building.

Walking around to the back, Kara spotted him stacking empty bottles in a tray. "Good afternoon," she said then walked over to help him.

"Oh, Kara! How's Harold?"

"That's what I'd like to find out, Bob."

The color rose in Bob's face as he turned from her to pick up another tray.

"I know you talked with Pops in the hospital. I also know he couldn't have killed Mr. Meyers."

His back was still towards her. "Don't ask me any questions. I promised not to talk."

"About what? You really don't believe Pops killed someone, do you?" She came around to face him.

Chapter 23

"No. Go away, Kara."

"Bob, I need to know!"

"Go away!" He hustled into the building without looking at her.

Great! She thought as she kicked at some stones. Just great! She thought about following him in. What did Pops tell Bob?

She would have to get the information out of him somehow, but the direct approach certainly wasn't working.

Kara walked down Lakeshore Road to Indian Rest Cabins. The police tape that previously had been around the cabins was gone. She went around and down to the private dock used by the guests. Standing on the end of the dock, she stared in the direction of Pops' house. From time to time, noises from parties at Indian Rest reached the Dyer house. Today there was a heavy haze and she wasn't able to see the house or the island. She stepped into one of the old rowboats, and putting her back into it, she rowed across. It took her just about an hour, including getting into the boat and tying it up at Pops' dock.

She rowed back to Indian Rest Cabins at a more relaxed speed, noticing the noise of the oars. She knew the conditions would be somewhat different before dawn. Rowing across in the dark wouldn't add too much time to someone who knew the lake like the back of his hand. Even if you didn't know the lake, the light out back was always on at the house so all you had to do was make a beeline for it. She could row back across the lake in the dark guided by the lights from the cabins without any problem. She definitely would have heard the sound of the oars.

She mentally ticked off the timeline. Pops was in the

kitchen at 3:35 a.m. drinking tea. He couldn't possibly have made it back by that time if the murder had happened after 3:15 a.m. Pops wasn't as strong as he used to be. It would have taken him much longer to make the trip. No! she thought. He couldn't have done it. She tied the boat to the Indian Rest dock and walked back up the road.

Lost in thought, she didn't notice the police cruiser pull up beside her. She startled, reaching around for her gun when Blake opened the door and said, "Need a ride?"

Kara moved her hand away from the holster and thought about ignoring him. She realized it wasn't his fault, but she had to have someone to blame and right now, it was Blake. She fought back an ugly retort and stopped.

"Blake, what are you doing here?"

"Asking if a friend needs a ride."

"You have a lot of nerve."

Blake's eyes shifted and his smile faded.

Kara remembered Pops telling her Blake was just doing his job. She could understand that. She had the scars that proved she understood having to do a job. Blake wasn't the guy to be wasting energy being angry with. She opened the door and looked at him.

"I admire nerve. I would love a ride back to the diner." She slid into the cruiser. "Thanks."

Blake moved his hat from the passenger seat. "Look, Kara, I know you're mad at me. Believe me, I understand why." He looked at the steering wheel. "I didn't want to arrest Harold, but I wasn't going to let a stranger do it." His voice trailed off. "Better me than someone else."

Kara felt her anger dissipate as she watched Blake. Twelve years her senior, he had been a good friend to the

<h1 align="center">Chapter 23</h1>

family over the years. Blake had practically lived at Pops' house when he was a kid. He was the one who brought the news of her father's death. She knew it was better for Pops to have a friend like Blake. She closed her hand over his. Blake's eyes shifted down to their clasped hands before snapping back to the road. Kara had caught the pain in his face as he turned to look out the side window.

Blake had always been a good friend. Kara was embarrassed she had been angry at him for doing his job. She sat still, giving him time to collect himself.

He shot a quick look at her before putting the cruiser into drive. It was several minutes before he spoke again.

"Not only does the timeline not work, but the markings on the bullets aren't even close to matching. It couldn't have been Harold's old antique that fired the bullets killing Meyers. I don't think he did it. I'm trying prove he's innocent. That stubborn old coot isn't making anything easier," Blake said. He turned to Kara. "I would guess that old thing hasn't been fired since he brought it home. Most of the guns folks have around here don't use those bullets, but it was that oddball type of bullet that killed Meyers. Harold did have a public spat with him. Since the argument, he's behaved kind of sneaky for several days. Then he made that," Blake paused. "Then he confessed. I can't deny he has a motive and we all know how protective he is of Wea Lake although I don't believe he'd kill someone over it. Blake shook his head. "Kara, at the very least, he's interfering with an investigation."

Kara sat still. The bullet marks didn't match his gun. "If they weren't fired from Pops' gun, could they be fired from another gun?"

Blake shook his head. "That bullet is specific to that weapon's caliber and rifling. The forensic guys were real excited to see a Nagant. They loved playing with that one. Good news is, it isn't the murder weapon. Bad news is, Harold lied."

"Pops didn't have any rounds for that gun anyway. It stayed in the case except when he showed someone."

"I know. He showed it to me once when I was a kid. Let me hold it. That's how I knew he had it. It was cool with the star and everything."

Kara only half-listened to Blake as her subconscious screamed at her; something about an antique gun; something about bullets. It buzzed inside her head like mosquitoes. "Blake, I kind of remember you can fire other ammunition from that gun. It wouldn't make the gas seal. You're sure it was the ammo that was made for that gun?"

"We're sure. We didn't find any of those bullets at Pops' house, so why would he confess?" Blake pulled into the back parking lot of the diner. "What possible motive?"

"Now that's the million-dollar question," Kara answered. "Both those old coots are shutting me out. I know they aren't going to talk to you if they won't talk to someone as cute as me." Kara opened the door, swinging her legs to the ground. "I'm going to find out."

"Kara, there's a murderer out there; it's dangerous." Kara threw a sharp look over her shoulder at Blake, causing him to throw up his hands.

"I know you know how to handle yourself, but you need to leave this to the professionals." Looking at the fire in her eyes, he knew what he said didn't matter. "Okay, okay,

Chapter 23

keep me in the loop. Don't do anything stupid, and don't tell anyone I gave you any information either. Nothing crazy, Kara! I mean it. I've had enough trouble from the Dyer's for this week."

Turning, she gave him a quick hug. "Thanks, Blake." Flashing a bright smile, she slid out of the cruiser, her feet crunching on the loose stone. "They can run, but they can't hide."

Blake shook his finger at her.

"Nothing crazy! Don't do anything until you talk with me first. Understand? You'll let me know if you find out anything, right, Kara?"

"Will do!"

Souvenirs

Chapter 24

Geneva, Kara, and Wes made a visit to Harold that evening. Harold continued to refuse to discuss the murder or his confession.

On the way back to the house, they picked up fish baskets from The Blue Gill then drove back to the house to eat.

"You know, we could drop a line in the lake. We could be eating fresh fish right about now," Wes said.

Kara laughed. "Are you saying The Blue Gill doesn't serve fresh fish?"

Wes ignored the question.

"I haven't been fishing in a while. I should plan to do that. What do you think, Kara?" Geneva smiled at Wes.

Kara looked up at her mom, who was gazing at Wes. She felt heat rushing to her face. To cover her embarrassment, she stuffed more onion rings into her mouth.

"I got an invite from Randy to go fishing with him Saturday. He said he found a new snag that's been productive and wants to try out his new rod and break in that underwater camera. I don't know if Saturday would be the best day for me, though."

Chapter 24

"Well, if we went during the week we could serve the fish as a special." Geneva smiled. "Fresh fish sounds nice."

Kara felt like a fifth wheel. It was kind of weird to see her mom flirting with Wes. Maybe she simply hadn't noticed it before. Her dad had been killed by a drunk driver years ago and her mom had started dating about three years later. None of the relationships ever lasted and Geneva had said she was giving up on the whole dating scene. To Kara's knowledge, she hadn't dated since. Wes was a few years younger than her mom and Kara had never considered him as a suitor for Geneva. Well, this is weird, she thought. "More lemonade, anyone?"

The weather had been sweltering all day, punctuated with bright, cloudless skies framing an unrelenting sun. The hot, humid air assaulted the wilting fields of sunflowers and soybeans, continuing long past sunset.

It had turned into one of those famous sticky Indiana nights. Kara got up once to change her sweat-soaked t-shirt, realizing the sticky heat wasn't the only thing keeping her awake. Sitting on the edge of her bed, she looked at the dresser drawer containing the sleeping pills the doc at the VA had prescribed to her. She rejected the medication and walked downstairs.

She made her way out to the end of the dock with a glass of milk while lightning flashed in the distant clouds. She strained to hear thunder rumbling, but the storm was still too far away to pick up the rolling booms. Kara welcomed the breeze sweeping across the lake, knowing the coming storm would bring respite from the heat.

Dangling her feet in the water, she sipped her milk and watched the lake surface transition from tiny ripples to a steady lapping against the dock.

"It wasn't Pops' gun." Kara said. She watched the lightning storm across the lake. "If it wasn't Pop's gun, why did he lie?" The breeze picked up. "The real question is who is he covering for?" The storm was approaching quickly with lightning illuminating the building thunderheads. The air around Kara began to fill with static from the coming storm.

She remained on the dock long after she finished the milk. The breeze became a steady wind as she continued to kick her feet in the lake water. Soon the effects of the warm milk produced a yawn. She kicked the water harder until it splashed up onto the dock. The breeze had become strong enough to blow her hair back from her face. There was thunder now.

Yawning once again, she decided to go inside to try to sleep. She drifted off listening to the cicadas' song and the percussion of thunder.

Smiling, Stan returned the phone to its cradle. With a satisfied expression, he rummaged around on his desk for the new file with the blank contract. He hummed tunes from "Fiddler on the Roof" while turning out the lights to his office then drove to his appointment, still humming.

Weather in Indiana is impacted by the agriculture, the Gulf of Mexico and the Great Lakes. The miles of fields of corn, wheat, soybeans, and sunflowers are heated by the summer sun. The plants reflect this heat, along with moisture, into the air. This hot, moisture-filled air then rises into the cooler cloud layers and is fed with more moisture from the Gulf and Lakes. An atmospheric war is waged as cooler air clashes with the heat. Moisture supplied by the rising air causes the clouds to form into large anvil-shaped thunderheads. These cooler giant cloud masses continue to compete with the warmer lower atmosphere. This battle in the ether produces destructive lightning storms with frequent hail events. The most deadly aspect of this war in the sky is the tornados that steamroll through the Midwest.

This destructive force was rolling nearer to Monroe when Stan pulled up in the driveway. Reaching for the folder beside him, he opened the car door. The thunder cracked and blinding lightning split the sky. Heavy rain appeared in a matter of seconds with a howling wind whipping the lake into whitecaps. The door of the house opened. Blinded by the light, Stan never saw the gun. The bullet hit him right between the eyes. He was still smiling as he fell backwards against his car.

Kara jerked awake from the sound of thunder crashing overhead. Quarter-sized hail pelted the house and the air itself seemed to be screaming. She was barely able to hear Monroe's storm alarms over the pounding of the hail. She ran from her room almost running into her mother, who was holding a flashlight. Without a word between them, they ran downstairs to the cellar. Kara could feel the wind charging through the living room. As the lightning flashed, she caught sight of a tree limb crashing through the window.

They hurried down into the storm cellar, Kara securing the walk-out door when all sound was sucked from the air. The swirling vortex of destruction was close to the house. When Kara opened the walk-out doors, they flew out of her hands. She could see the kitchen door banging mutely in the torrent of wind. The tornado was pulling everything into it, including sound.

Kara climbed out of the storm cellar to take a look. The lightning flashed as the sound of a train rushed by her house and the funnel cloud moved out to the lake. She could feel her mother pulling on her shirt. She knew the capricious nature of these storms meant it could quickly turn and come roaring back at her. She understood the danger. The funnel cloud, now a tower of spinning lake water, was awesome to witness against the backdrop of the lightning. The stinging hail pelted her as she stood, awestruck. "Kara Dyer! Get back in here immediately!" her mother yelled over the storm. Sound had returned. Kara moved back into the cellar.

"Kara Louise, what did you think you were doing?"

"Watching the show."

They sat in the basement, waiting for the alarms to stop sounding.

"Might as well see the damage," Geneva said.

"I think some tree limbs crashed into the living room," Kara said.

The only real damage was one broken window and a wet rug. The lawn chairs were gone. The rowboat, full of melting ice pellets, was still attached securely to the dock. Though freshly dented by hail, both cars were still in the driveway. They took time to cover the broken window and dress before they left to check on the diner.

The Yellow Dog was outfitted with a large generator so people could still be fed in situations like this.

As they drove down the road, Geneva grabbed Kara's arm. "Will you look at that!" Geneva pointed to the place where the Wilkes farm had been. In the lightning,

Chapter 24

they could see it had all been reduced to a pile of rubble. Kara turned the car around to head to the farm. Detouring around downed power lines as well as dead livestock blocking the road, they managed to pull into the driveway. In the remaining lightning they could see the farm had been leveled.

Geneva was out of the car before Kara put it in park. Running toward where she thought the storm cellar was, Geneva frantically cleared debris.

"Merciful Lord, please let them be alright!" Geneva cried. "Kara, the walkout for the storm cellar is under here, I think. Help me get it cleared off!"

"Mom, take my phone!" Geneva continued to pull off pieces of metal. "Mom, stop! You're not helping! Call 911! Kara thrust the phone at Geneva. "Call them now!"

Geneva stared at the phone before taking it from Kara, who was flinging pieces of wood and metal. "Hurry, honey! They might be trapped down there."

Kara moved to the area Geneva had indicated and hauled larger pieces of tin roofing from the area.

Kara heard banging. "Hello, anyone down there?" The banging increased. Ignoring the pulling from her burn scars, she heaved away hunks of sheetrock, intermixed with shattered furniture. She paused again to listen to what sounded like a dog.

"Mom, I hear someone!"

Geneva ran over. "Anyone there?" Geneva dropped down, digging at the muddy ground. "Here! The door is here!"

Kara moved more debris away until she could see the walkout door. Not bothering to remove more litter, they pulled on the door together until it opened. The family dog darted out, barking loudly.

"Geneva, you're a sight for sore eyes!" exclaimed Edna Wilkes as she emerged from the shelter.

The emergency vehicles arrived about ten minutes later. The Wilkes' were all alive and unharmed, but the family farm was obliterated. Only one wall still remained along with the first floor of the century-old farm house. The silos and newer barns were gone. The stone walls of the original barn still stood.

The relief of being rescued quickly dissipated when the family viewed what was left of a once productive business. Not even one live chicken was found.

Chapter 25

Kara pulled down what was left of the front awning at the diner. Other than that, it was in excellent shape. They fired up the generator and checked for damage before turning on the grill. Kara started pots of coffee, hot chocolate, and water for tea before the first responders began arriving. Geneva set out the open sign when she unlocked the front door.

Wes came in about ten minutes later, just as Kara started a pot of oatmeal. When the rescue crew brought the first of the tornado victims into the diner, they were greeted by warm coffee and hot cereal.

Mr. Wilkes wanted to stay with the farm in case any of the livestock had survived and returned. It took some time for the rescue team to convince him he wasn't going to be able to see anything until morning. The fire chief himself had driven Mr. and Mrs. Wilkes to the diner. Volunteers with blankets and dry clothes came in from all over.

When Edna Wilkes arrived, she threw her arms around Geneva. "Oh, Gennie we lost everything, everything! We only found one of the pigs alive. Tom had to use Blake's gun to kill it. Everything is gone!" she sobbed.

"Edna, you're all still alive. Your family will rebuild

everything else," Geneva said softly. "You will, the same way families around here always have."

Geneva held Edna, looking around at the other people there. The Wilkes' had lost so much. Electricity was out everywhere and most had some damage to their property. Bob's old maple tree had been tossed through his garage roof. Here they all were, gathered at the diner to regroup.

Wes made biscuits, gravy, scrambled eggs, and bacon. He pulled several trays of cinnamon rolls out of the fridge to bake while Kara ran around filling the rescue workers' thermoses with coffee. She made certain folks shivering at the tables had hot food. She sat the water for the Wilkes' dog on the floor before noticing that Mitch Wilkes was sitting apart from the rest of the family.

Poor kid, she thought. First he gets grounded for life, now this. Kara went back to the kitchen to pour a couple cups of hot chocolate, one for the teenager, and one for herself. She put a mug in front of Mitch.

"Thanks."

Kara smiled as she sat down, watching Mitch stare down at the table top. She knew sometimes all that was needed was to know someone else was there. Mitch picked up the mug to drink the chocolate and when he set it back down, she placed her hand on his arm. He jerked away, fighting back tears.

"Mitch, it's okay." Kara pulled him into her arms as he cried. Suddenly, he stopped and glanced around, wiping his eyes with the back of his hand.

Kara smiled at him.

He dropped his head. "Thank you."

She ruffled his hair. "You want to help out here tonight? Not all the usual crew can make it in."

He gave her a startled look. "Sure. What do I do?"

"Know how to fry eggs?"

Wes gave Kara a wink when she presented Mitch as an expert egg-fryer. She went to the oven to check on the latest batch of cinnamon rolls while Wes handed Mitch the spatula and explained to the young man what to do. Kara waited until Wes nodded before heading out to the dining room with a fresh pot of coffee.

At dawn, the rescue workers regrouped at the fire station. Now that they could see what the damage was, they could make plans. Most of them ended up at the diner for breakfast. Geneva hadn't opened the cash register once. Mitch was doing pretty well, considering he just learned how to cook eggs. It certainly was taking his mind off the loss his family had suffered. Kara even caught him smiling.

Spotting Wes and Kara at the counter, Blake walked over "Harold and the jail are fine," he said.

"I should have broken him out during the storm! I didn't think of it. Darn!" Wes said. Kara grimaced, but Blake just laughed.

"How is the Wilkes' place?"

"Leveled. Barn, silos, and house. All the animals are either dead or have run off. Most of the equipment is badly damaged. Good news is, the fields made it okay for the most part. There will be a harvest."

"Is the family still here?" Blake looked around the room.

"No, I think they left with friends. Mitch is still here, though. We've got him flipping eggs. He isn't bad. He's only fifteen, but I think Mom's going to hire him. He's going to stay with us at the house until the family gets things together."

"You guys always did take in every puppy dog that came along."

Seeing Blake at the counter, Geneva moved over to the group and said, "You were once a puppy, too, if I remember. This isn't charity; it's business. We need good egg-flippers."

"Uh-huh." Blake held out his thermos and grinned.

Things stayed crazy busy until noon when electricity was restored to the diner. By evening, The Blue Gill and Dot's were up and running. Geneva kept the diner open late so people could have some supper. It was about 8 p.m. when they got home.

"Kara, take Mitch up to Harry's room and get him some clothes," Geneva whispered as she wearily climbed the stairs to her room.

Chapter 26

The next morning, Kara pounded on the bedroom door. "Mitch, wake up! Time to earn your keep!" she shouted.

"What?"

"Get up! Time to go to work! We're going to open this morning. Don't tell me they let you sleep in at the farm?"

Geneva had already left for the jail by the time Mitch made it downstairs to the kitchen.

"There are hot muffins on the table. If you want more breakfast, you'll have to cook it yourself when we get to work." Kara pushed a glass of milk in Mitch's direction.

"You guys get up before my dad does," Mitch complained.

"How does it feel to be a working stiff?" Kara said.

"I worked on the farm."

"You were up early the other day when you walked home. You should have let Randy drive you to your farm instead of walking."

"What?" His brow was wrinkled. "What are you talking about? I didn't see Randy."

"You should have let Randy drive you home. He saw

139

you on Lakeshore Road. You didn't take his offer."

"I never saw Randy. I wasn't on Lakeshore. I was heading home, not toward town. I didn't see any cars. I wasn't so out of it I wouldn't have remembered Randy offering me a lift. That's a long walk."

"No one came along asking if you wanted a ride?"

"No." Kara might have had two heads and announced she was from Mars the way Mitch looked at her.

"Do you know what time you got home?"

"Right before 5:00. Why?"

"Randy would have been finished with his route before then." Kara spoke more to herself than to Mitch.

"What?"

"Nothing. You finished with your milk?" Mitch held up the empty glass, still giving Kara a puzzled look. "Good. Help me clean up these dishes."

When Randy pushed his fishing boat away from the dock, it was already dawn. A couple of sharp pulls on the small Johnson motor was all that was needed to grind it into life. He motored to his favorite spot and cast with his brand new Shimano reel. He was smiling at the fish jumping from the water, chasing the insects buzzing over the surface. "Yep, a storm always does make for good fishing."

Squinting into the rising sun, he figured he'd get in a couple of hours of good fishing and have time to get some underwater photographs of the fish shelters before he had to go to work at the John Deere dealership. He motored out to an old snag that was inside the mouth of the inlet. The storm had stirred things up a bit and Randy wanted to see if the snag would produce anything today.

It didn't take him long to have a string of bass on the

Chapter 26

line. "Well worth the money," he said, putting his new rod and reel down in the boat. He checked the position of the sun. "Lots of time." The Johnson motor sputtered without firing off. Randy made a few adjustments and pulled again. The motor coughed into life and Randy maneuvered the little boat toward one of the fish shelters.

The lake was still. Only the sound of the trolling motor broke the quiet of the morning. The glassy surface was marred by the wake of the boat. Randy dropped anchor at the approximate location of the nearest group of shelters. He took a few moments to play with the underwater camera housing before putting on his snorkeling gear. He took one last look around to make certain this was the place before sliding into the water.

Close enough to the shore to attract the smaller fish, Randy swam into the shelters where they zipped in and out. There was already a lot of vegetation growing on the structures. Cool! These are going to be fantastic shots! Randy thought as he swam, returning to the surface from time to time for air and to align himself with his boat.

He swam over to the last of the shelters and noticed an oddly-shaped object close to shore. As he swam toward it, the shadow of a boat passed over his head. Randy looked up at the passing craft before continuing to swim toward the shape. As he neared, he came to an abrupt halt. It was a car. Randy wondered how it had been missed when the shelters were dropped there. Boy! thought Randy. Is Harold ever going to be mad! He's not going to be happy this litter is so close to the fish shelters. As Randy swam closer to take a photo, he suddenly recognized the car. It belonged to Stan.

Randy snapped off a couple of quick shots and

surfaced then took some shots of the area so he could locate it again, knowing he would have to tell Blake about all this. Randy swam toward his small fishing boat. He thought, I had to leave my phone in the car.

He pulled himself into the boat and fired off the motor, heading in a direct line to town. After a few moments, he noticed another fisherman on the lake and changed direction, thinking the other fisherman might have a phone.

Pulling closer, Randy shouted, "Ahoy!" and waved as he approached the other craft. "Hey, there! Do you have a phone on you? A car that belongs to a guy I know is in the lake over there. We need to call the police!"

"Phone? Yeah, I have a phone. Car in the lake, you say?"

"Yeah! I got some photographs, but we need to call the police."

"Photographs? Of the car?"

"Yeah, you want to see them?"

Chapter 27

Kara had been waiting for Randy to come in for breakfast. Mid-morning, Geneva and Blake walked in with Harold. Kara threw her arms around her grandfather, whooping for joy.

"Pops, what? Why? Did Mom break you out?"

"Kara, you're squeezing the breath out of me, let go honey!" Harold laughed as he squeezed her in return.

Blake stood to one side, shuffling his feet. Kara asked, "Blake, did you have anything to do with this?"

Blake answered modestly, "The evidence showed Harold's gun wasn't used and, as we both know, he couldn't have gotten over there and back in time. I don't think anyone was serious about pressing charges," Blake glared at Harold, "He did interfere with a police investigation, though."

Kara released her hold on Harold to throw her arms around Blake. "Thank you so much." She planted a kiss on Blake's cheek that left him blushing.

Wes came flying out of the kitchen and starting shaking Harold's hand. "Do you have any prison tattoos?" Wes asked with a wink.

The few folks still at the diner closed in a tight circle

around Harold before Geneva took him and Mitch home. Kara and Wes closed up the diner a little early, but Kara didn't go straight home. She wanted to talk to Randy and made her way down the street to the John Deere dealership.

"Kara, you wanting to buy a tractor?" Beth Raines smiled at Kara from behind the repair counter.

"No, that one Pops bought about a hundred years ago is still going strong."

"I keep telling the rep, but they don't listen to me. They just make them too good." Beth walked out from behind the counter and shook Kara's hand.

"I heard Harold is in jail for killing that man at the cabins."

"Not anymore. They just let him out today. Mom and Blake brought him home. He confessed, for some weird reason. It looks like I wasn't the only one who didn't believe him."

"Well, now; that doesn't sound like Harold."

"He's not talking and I don't know why he said he was the murderer," Kara said.

Beth patted her hand. "Your mother must be happy to have the old goat back home. Randy said the other day he couldn't have done it because there just wasn't enough time." Beth frowned. "I sure would like to know why he confessed."

Kara suppressed a smile. People talking would provide her with the answers she needed. "I don't know, but you can bet I'm going to make him tell me."

Beth nodded her head. "I suppose you will. I just don't think the old softy could have killed anyone! How's he doing?"

Chapter 27

"I don't know. Mom stopped by the diner before she took him home. Wes and I stayed to close up." Kara said, "He looked embarrassed. I don't think he said a dozen words," Kara paused and looked toward the workshop. "I'm here looking for Randy. He around?"

Beth looked up at the clock.

"Randy? Nope. The scamp didn't call in either. I don't know where he is. Probably out fishing. He always thinks the fishing is good after a big storm. He was going on about some secret spot," Beth frowned. "He did talk about using that fancy new underwater camera of his to get some shots of the fish shelters for the Association."

Kara threw her hands up in the air and grinned. "Maybe I'll try to find private site this afternoon. He might be right about the fishing."

"Well, if you find him tell him he's fired. Also tell him to get himself in tomorrow as soon as he can. I have a couple of mowers folks need to have repaired."

Kara laughed as Beth sighed. "It's a sad thing to have to make idle threats. He's the best mechanic I've ever seen. When he gets older someone is going to hire him away from me, I just know it."

"If he does come in, can you let him know I need to talk to him?"

"Sure will. But he fixes the mowers first before he goes off to see you!"

"Fair enough!"

Kara cornered her grandfather upon her return to the house. "Pops, what were you thinking?"

"I missed you, too, Little Bit." Harold grinned at her.

Kara planted her fists on her hips. "Why?"

Souvenirs

Harold's expression underwent several changes in rapid succession, from amusement, to embarrassment, to what appeared to be a thunderstorm. "Kara, that's my business. I'm sorry I put you through this. I have a good reason and you don't need to know what it is. End of discussion, little girl." He turned on his heel and strode off.

Little Girl! She had to fight the urge to stamp her foot. Little girl, indeed! She thought about running after him, but heard his truck start up. She did stamp her foot before flopping down on the couch.

Geneva called from the kitchen, "Kara, are you still here? Did I hear Pop's truck leaving?"

"Yeah, Mom, it's me, and yes, Pops just left."

Mitch came downstairs and grabbed the channel changer. "You watching that?"

Kara looked over at him and said, "Mitch, you want to come fishing with me?"

"No. Wish I could. Ms. Dyer is going to drop me off at the farm. I'm going to help my folks start cleaning up. Going fishing sounds like a lot more fun."

Kara said, "Well, we'll have fish for dinner tonight."

Kara found Geneva in the kitchen. She gave her mom a quick kiss and said, "I should be back around 6 p.m."

"Take your hat. Your nose is getting sunburned!"

Kara had some trouble getting the trolling motor to fire off. Randy needs to take a look at this piece of junk, she thought. When the engine finally started, she took a course between the shore and the island. From time to time, she idled the engine to drop a line in the water until she reached the inlet. The lakeshore narrowed enough here that a small boat barely fit through, opening onto a good-sized pool. The

146

entrance was overhung with tree branches and was hard to see unless you knew the area.

Kara was delighted when she first discovered it as a child. She thought it was a secret place all her own, but everyone in Monroe knew about it. It just wasn't that popular because it wasn't accessible by road. There was an overgrown path from the road on the south side, but the best way to get there was by boat.

Kara wasn't having much luck with fish. Her main interest was locating Randy anyway. The casual line drops she made weren't producing even a nibble. She killed the motor and rowed through the narrows, ducking beneath the branches. She didn't see any evidence of Randy there. As she rowed out, she saw a fishing rod stuck in the bracken floating against the shore. Using her fishing net, she pulled it toward her, discovering Randy's name burned into the handle. This must be the fancy new rod he had been bragging about.

She paused, looking around. She still didn't see any other sign of him and she knew for a fact he wouldn't have left his new rod. Putting it in her boat, she coaxed the motor to life and with a heightened sense of unease, she continued southward, intently scanning the shore and the lake.

Kara slowly made her way down the shoreline, approaching what the locals called the "Shaman's Finger", a small hook of exceptionally swampy land extending from the southeast end of the lake and curving towards the west. It created a dark pungent place that nearly all the kids, and even some adults, believed was haunted by the ghost of an Indian shaman. Even as a child, Kara had not been afraid of the area. She just thought it smelled funny. Now she understood it was just the lake doing the job of cleaning itself. Like the pool, it was only accessible by foot through the woods and by boat, and was overhung with willow trees and choked with brambles. There was a boat bouncing gently against the shore under one of the willows.

"Hello! Randy, you around somewhere?" Her voice sounded flat against the dead air in the overgrown inlet. She killed the engine and rowed up to the other boat, wondering if some kid had just abandoned it or had left it untied. As she got closer, she noticed the flies and increased her efforts.

There Randy was, lying in the boat, his hair matted with blood. Flies crawled all over his face. Smelling the blood, she jumped out of her boat and waded over to him. With urgency, she brushed the flies away and pressed two fingers against his neck. She could feel the slight pulse; he was alive. "Randy?" He didn't respond. His face was ashen; his breath shallow. "Oh, Randy, what happened to you?"

She looked around, cursing herself for leaving her phone at home. She didn't want to move him. She could carry him to the road, but then what? Still standing in the water, she grabbed Randy's boat and dragged it toward hers, then tied the two boats together. The engine to her boat wouldn't even turn over. Turning to Randy's boat, she attempted to start that engine. It sputtered, coughed and then died.

"Randy, I could use you right now." She tried Randy's engine again, but it just wouldn't fire. Panic rose in her like a tide. She jumped back into the water then pulled herself into her boat. Grabbing the oars, she rowed like crazy for Pops' dock.

The paramedics said Randy was in a coma and in

Chapter 27

pretty bad shape. Dr. Marr told her he wouldn't have made it much longer out in the heat. They were able to get him out of the row boat and on to the stretcher faster than Kara thought possible. He was already in the ambulance when Blake arrived.

Standing on the dock, Kara felt sick. It was the smell of the blood in the hot air. Funny how it smells the same no matter where you are, she thought dully. She'd never forget that smell. It had clung to her skin ever since that day in the desert and was now being resurrected here at home. She almost heard the sounds of the groans and cries of the wounded. She could see the faces, the color of death. Only now she couldn't hear the gun fire for some reason. She seemed to be able to hear the convoy's attackers moving in for the kill, but no guns. She was visibly shaking when Blake found her on the end of the dock staring at the rowboat.

He had talked with the paramedics before looking for Kara, finally finding her here on the dock. She was sweating so much her shirt was clinging to her back. He saw that the motor was tipped up in both boats, and the oars were askew. She rowed the whole way here, he thought.

"Kara, did the motor quit?" He walked up behind her and placed his hand on her shoulder.

Kara didn't hear Blake approach or hear him talking. She wasn't hearing anything but the sound of approaching death. She grabbed his arm and spun, kicking out and knocking him off his feet. Blake sprawled backwards on the dock, amazed at the change in the girl he had known since childhood. She was on him in an instant; pupils dilated, her eyes completely black.

"Kara, it's me, Blake! You know, the local cop!"

Souvenirs

He was shouting at her as he tried to protect his face and restrain her at the same time. "What are you doing?"

Her dark eyes seemed to come back from far away as a light of awareness flickered in them.

"Kara, it's just me." He had grabbed her arms and was holding her tight. She blinked at him then drew in a ragged breath as her head turned, taking in the house.

Blake pushed her off his chest. "That was some kick. Wow, do you move fast! You sure don't hit like a girl!" He felt his side. "I think I'm going to bruise. I could arrest you for that." He paused. She just proved she was a whole lot more dangerous than he had thought. "Or maybe I should hire you as my new deputy."

She breathed again. Rolling up to a squatting position on the dock, she fought waves of nausea.

He sat up beside her. "Last time a girl beat me up I was in second grade."

She leaned over the dock and threw up.

He looked at the pain reflected in her eyes. There was so much emotion buried there. He approached and squatted down beside her. "Kara, you're back at home now. It's okay."

She pulled herself back to a sitting position, wiped off her mouth with the back of her hand, and looked over at him. "Blake, someone tried to kill Randy."

"Looks that way. You want to tell me how you found him?" He looked at both boats.

"Randy thought there would be good fishing after the storm. I went looking for him because I wanted to talk to him about the person he saw the night Hollis was killed. I took my tackle with me." She paused rubbing her face. "I found that new rod of his stuck in the brambles by the little pool, but didn't find him. So I continued down the shore looking for him when I saw his boat in the Finger. It could have drifted there. Everything eventually drifts that way." She glared at the boats. "Or someone left him there because no one ever goes there."

"Yeah, loose stuff on the lake does end up there. It would take a while for a boat to drift over there."

Kara continued to glare at the boat. Blake looked at her closely, noticing how pale she was. "Kara, let's go in and get some water. I'm kind of hot out here." He stood holding out a hand to her. She didn't take it right away, but after her first unsteady attempt at standing, she let him help her up.

Chapter 28

Blake was making Kara tea when Harold walked in. "What's that smell?" He looked at Kara. "Blake, I saw an ambulance leaving. What's going on?"

"Kara found Randy unconscious in his boat. It had drifted into the Finger. Looks like someone hit him on the head."

Harold whistled. "Why would anyone want to hurt Randy?"

Kara looked up at Harold, her eyes smoldering. "The real question is what did he know that would cause anyone to want to kill him?" She was moving the toothpicks into different designs.

"You think it has something to do with Hollis?"

"Yeah, I do!" Kara snapped. "It has something to do with Mitch not seeing Randy that morning." Kara looked at Blake.

Harold looked around. "Where is everyone else?"

Blake said, "Mitch and Geneva are doing clean-up at Wilkes' farm."

Harold said, "Oh, yeah. Gennie did tell me that. I should go over, too."

"Maybe we'd better go get him," Kara said. "Come

Chapter 28

on, Blake, are you just going to stand around brewing tea all day?"

As they drove alongside the fields, Kara could smell the rich aroma of corn change to acrid smoke as they neared the Wilkes' farm. The smoke rising from the burn pit filled the air with a thick sooty smoke. Kara's hand covered her face as her eyes squinted closed. "Oh my lands, what is that?"

Blake grimaced as he rolled up the windows. "The state health guy was up. He said the best way to handle all the dead livestock was to dig a burn pit. The volunteer firemen used some loaned construction equipment to do the job." He wrinkled his nose. "I guess they have the fire going now."

Kara coughed. "I guess so. Boy, does that stink!"

A red sports coupe passed them, going in the opposite direction.

Blake's eyebrows went up. "Isn't that the Olson kid? Didn't think he would be the type to get his hands dirty. Must be why he's leaving."

"Yeah, It is Mike Olson." Kara turned to look back at the coupe.

Blake pulled the cruiser into the driveway as Kara shook her head. "Holy smoke! Now that I can see the damage, there is nothing left. Except for a wall and part of that old barn, everything is just gone," Kara said.

"Everything here was right in the path," Blake said.

Kara noted there were three distinct groups of townspeople at the site. One group appeared to be salvaging through the rubble. The second group was collecting rubbish and dumping it into the burn pit. The third seemed

Souvenirs

to just be gawking.

Heavy construction equipment was parked where the small barn used to stand. Volunteer firemen were working around the burn pit. Carcasses of dead animals were visible through the flames and smoke as were the building's remains. The smoke was pervasive and Kara was glad the wind was blowing to the Northeast across the fields. It took a while to find Mitch among the throng of people moving around the site.

"Wow! What is that? Eau du stinky swamp water? You fall in while you were fishing or something? You smell real bad," Mitch commented.

Kara smelled her shoulder and wrinkled her nose. "Something like that. I'm surprised you would notice in all this smoke."

Mitch stepped back from her. "I don't see how you couldn't notice that stench."

Kara sniffed her shoulder again and laughed. "See what you mean. At least I don't have to worry about the smoke ruining my clothes."

Kara turned, scanning the area to see who was close by.

"So what are you doing? Clearing or salvaging?"

"Oh, salvaging. Mom wants me to try to find any photographs. Besides I don't want to get close to that fire pit. It smells almost as bad as you."

Kara snorted and rubbed soot off Mitch's face. "You're not exactly a rose garden."

Smiling, she said, "I'll help you. You got an extra pair of gloves? Where do I start?"

As she worked, her eyes continued to sweep over the

other people. She looked for any person or thing that didn't fit.

Kara helped Mitch move some tin roofing to a pile of salvage material while keeping an eye on the other folks who were helping out. Frustrated by all the mess, she focused on just the people nearby. This wasn't a good situation for spotting someone behaving suspiciously. With all the grime- covered faces, it was difficult to recognize anyone.

I just can't believe any of these folks would kill anyone. They're out here taking on this horrible job just to help out a neighbor, Kara thought as she studied Mitch. I've got to protect him. The problem is I just don't know who from. Kara looked around again, squinting to see through the smoke.

She thought just about everyone in town was there, even the ones who were just there for the show had tied something across their faces to keep out the smoke, making it even more difficult to see who was who.

"Wow, look at that car!" Mitch was pointing at Mike's red coupe as it pulled away, the low afternoon sun glinting off its perfect curves.

"That's the guy who moved into the Olson farm, isn't it? What a nice ride!"

"Yeah, it's a honey." She poked him in the arm. "Mitch, let's go over and get something to drink."

They walked to the table set up with water, coffee and lemonade.

"Did I just see Mike Olson drive away?"

"Oh, yeah. Nice guy. Kind of fancy though. Found a pig on a back road and brought it here."

Souvenirs

"Really, a dead pig? He put it in his car?"

"No. Well, sort of. He was here earlier and said he had seen the pig. I offered to go get it, but he said he would take care of it. He wrapped it in an old carpet so it wouldn't ruin his car. I've been hauling dead hogs and cattle around all day so I gave him a hand getting it to the pit. It was a small pig. All we needed was a wheelbarrow to haul it."

"Really? That's not what I would expect from him," said Kara, puzzled. She scanned the scene again. Too many people had been walking around to see who was and wasn't there. She still didn't think Mike was the kind of guy to engage in offensive work like this, especially moving dead animals.

Bob and Dottie showed up right at dusk with sandwiches, soda, and ice cream. Kara did a walk around with Mitch where they could see that most of the debris had been removed or at least organized. The fire pit was going to smolder all night with the firemen directing work with the backhoe to make sure it wasn't going to be a threat to anyone. Most of the people had gone home by the time the fire pit was filled in.

Kara jabbed Mitch in the arm. "You get to ride back in the cruiser with me and Blake. I'll ask Blake to run the lights for you. Won't that be fun?"

Mitch's face went blank as he raised an eyebrow in response to Kara's comments. "I don't know if I'll be able to withstand the smell of Ms. Swamp Water. You still smell worse than that fire does." He grimaced, causing the dirt covering his face to crack.

Kara laughed and said, "Blake probably won't let either one of us in the cruiser."

Chapter 28

Blake made them sit on blankets in the back.

"So, what did happen to you? Honestly, you really do smell like you fell in the swamp!"

"Yeah, about that," Blake said.

Kara looked up to see Blake's eyes fixed on her in the rearview mirror.

"Kara found Randy on the lake. He had a head injury and was unconscious in his boat. She rowed both boats back to Harold's from the finger."

"Oh, man! Is Randy okay?" Mitch asked.

"He's stable, but still unconscious," Blake answered. His eyes went to Kara.

"Good thing you found him! Sorry about the swamp water remarks," Mitch said.

Kara punched him on the shoulder and they playfully scuffled in the back seat.

"Children, children! Behave or I won't turn on the lights!"

Geneva arrived home well after Mitch and Kara. She had stayed with the Wilkes family until everyone had gone.

Chapter 29

After Mitch had gone to bed, Kara told Geneva about Randy.

"Well, it doesn't seem there's going to be an end to this for some time," Geneva said. "Are you certain Randy was attacked?"

"Pretty sure. Even Randy doesn't know it wasn't Mitch he saw. The only ones who know are Mitch and probably the guy who killed Hollis. I'm worried about Mitch."

Geneva nodded her head. "I take it Mitch doesn't know all the details about Randy."

Kara shook her head. "No reason to upset the poor kid. He has enough to deal with now. We just need to keep an eye on him. It's a good thing he's staying with us."

"I'll talk with Wes tomorrow so he can watch over Mitch, too," Geneva said.

"Speaking of which, I have a plan. Mom, you sleep in tomorrow. I'll open."

"What plan, Kara? You aren't doing anything silly, are you?"

"Nope, just going to encourage the gossip. You not being there first thing will help it along."

Chapter 29

Geneva rolled her eyes. "Well, I wouldn't mind sleeping in, but don't you get a brawl started. We've had enough drama around here for a lifetime!"

Kara woke up early to make breakfast. After Mitch finished eating, they headed over to the diner.

As always, Saturday was busy. Wes kept Mitch and the rest of the cooks hopping in the kitchen. Kara felt like her legs were being run off even though the extra weekend wait staff was all there. When her Mom came in at 8 a.m., Kara was more than happy to see her.

She was sitting just inside the kitchen with a glass of water when Blake walked in the kitchen door. Wes was in the middle of scrambling eggs and slowly turned to face Blake. "I confess; it's true. I use Lake Michigan seagulls instead of chicken. I feel so much better now that I don't have to hide anymore. Take me away, Officer." Wes put his head down and held out his hands, waiting to be taken into custody.

Blake said, "I've eaten your chicken and I believe it. And as compelling as your confession is, I'm just not that interested."

"Oh, you believe me so easily? Just you wait. You'll pay for your lack of respect," Wes exclaimed as he waved his spatula at Blake. "You ain't seen nothing yet."

"That's what I'm afraid of." Blake turned to Kara. "How's Mitch doing?"

Kara looked quickly over at Mitch who was busy burning his hands as he took biscuits out of the oven. She whispered, "No attempts on his life, if that's what you mean." Turning to Mitch she commented, "I think he has potential." She grinned at Wes.

Souvenirs

"Yeah, but does he have tattoos?" Wes shoveled eggs onto a plate with some bacon and walked toward Mitch. "Hey, big Fella, you ever considered getting a tattoo?"

Blake looked around the kitchen and stepped out into the dining room. "Kara, let's take a walk."

"Wes, I'm stepping out a minute."

They walked out back to the cruiser. "Kara, this is what the state boys have discovered." He handed her some printouts.

She read through them, reading that Randy had a skull fracture as a result of being hit on the head. Kara looked up at Blake, "Well, duh! Of course, he was hit on the head!" Blake frowned and Kara went back to reading. "Outside of Pops owning that type of gun, his public row with Hollis, and of course his confession that he did it, there's nothing to tie him to the murder," she laughed as she handed the papers back to Blake.

He frowned at the paper. "I think Randy saw the person who killed Hollis. The problem is only you and I know it wasn't Mitch who Randy thought he saw. Randy doesn't even know that."

Kara walked back toward the dumpster. Frowning, she pushed a stone around with her foot. "I'm still wondering why Pops said he killed Mr. Meyers. He still won't talk to me."

"Harold has to be protecting someone."

Kara looked at Blake. Something was tickling at the back of her memory like a well-loved bedtime story. She kept thinking, Pops is protecting someone. He thinks he knows something. She tried to focus on what Blake was saying. Something in her head was demanding her

Chapter 29

attention.

"Kara, someone is out there killing people. There's something I'm missing. Things just don't fit. Hollis is a complete stranger to the area. From everything I found out, he's a decent guy. No real enemies lurking out there just waiting to do him in. It's just a shame the bullets were the same type used in Harold's old souvenir pistol."

Kara jerked. Something about guns; an old story. She'd heard the story all her life and no longer paid close attention at the retelling. When Pops came back from the war he brought that gun and Bob back with him. She caught her breath and almost shouted. "They were in the same squad together!"

"What?" Blake had been watching Kara closely. He studied her face, watching her memory surface. He realized he was holding his breath, afraid any sound would interrupt her train of thought.

Kara's head was humming. She was remembering the story that now was only occasionally retold. Pops returning from Korea. The joke about Bob being in his backpack. Bob was the only child of older parents. His parents had died before the war. After it was over, he didn't have any place to go. He came home temporarily with Pops to figure out what he wanted to do and never left. They both had brought back the same souvenir, the same type of weapon used by North Korean soldiers during the war. Pops' gun had the star; Bob's didn't. "Bob has one!" She grabbed Blake's arm, her face flushed and eyes glowing. "Bob has one of those guns! Pops is protecting Bob!"

Blake whistled under his breath. "You're right! I've heard that story a dozen times." Blake squinted. "You know,

Souvenirs

I passed Bob that morning around 3 a.m., just short of the turn-off to the cabins. He said he had a flat tire."

"But why would Bob kill Mr. Meyers?"

"He may not have. He did have the spare on the car and was putting something away in his trunk. Of course, he was pretty mad."

"Bob was angry with Stan and Mr. Meyers because they had upset Pops. Bob isn't the most forgiving guy, but murder?"

Blake nodded his head in agreement and met her gaze. "Harold and Bob would do anything for each other."

Kara was silent. She knew the truth of Blake's statement. They would do anything for each other. She just couldn't believe either one of them had the capacity for murder.

"We've got to make Pops talk." Kara voice was urgent. "He thinks he's doing the right thing by trying to protect Bob."

"First, we're not going to do anything. Second, I'm going to go talk with Bob. If he has the gun, I'm going to get it one way or another."

"Great! I'll tell Mom I'm going to be gone for a while."

Blake chided, "Like I said, Kara, we're not going to do anything."

"So, you think Bob is just going to talk to you?"

"No, Kara." His mouth was rigid.

She crossed her arms across her chest. "I can beat you up."

"I can arrest you, missy." His angry tone was one he had used effectively on others.

Chapter 29

She giggled. "Missy?"

Blake dropped his head. He knew then he had lost the argument. "Yeah, Missy," he smiled.

Kara grinned and giggled again. "I can still beat you up."

Kara may have been smiling and her eyes twinkling, but Blake couldn't mistake the set of her shoulders. He knew she wasn't backing off. After yesterday afternoon, he knew this smiling imp before him actually could beat him up. She moved fast when she attacked, Blake remembered as he rubbed his head. "Okay, Missy, I do all the talking. Agreed?"

"Yep."

"I'm serious about this. You talk, this never happens again."

"Scout's honor."

"You were never a scout."

Souvenirs

Chapter 30

Kara pulled Wes and her mom aside and asked them to keep a close eye on Mitch before she left with Blake. She wasn't interested in seeing the same color in Mitch's face that she had seen in Randy's.

On the way down to The Blue Gill, Kara wondered why Pops would think Bob had killed Hollis. She knew Bob wasn't happy Pops had been upset by Hollis and Stan. Most of the people who had witnessed it felt the same way. Bob also may not have known Pops and Mr. Meyers had talked later. She just couldn't believe he would kill someone just because Pops had argued with them. There wouldn't be anyone left in Monroe. Pops tended to express his views freely and passionately.

Kara smiled when she thought about all the old guys eating breakfast or hanging out at The Bait and Tackle Shop or spending evenings at The Blue Gill. Most of these guys had known each other since birth. They all spent their time puffing up like roosters, feathers flying as they sorted out the world's problems. She loved to listen to them talk, laughing at their comments and learning that some things never change.

These were the people who were part of the fabric

and texture of Wea Lake. Her mind rambled over the small population of Monroe. She just couldn't imagine any one of them murdering a complete stranger just because Pops lost his temper. She just couldn't imagine any of them trying to kill Randy for any reason. There had to be more. Like Blake, she knew she was missing something that was right in front of her.

Blake pulled into the parking lot of The Blue Gill. They hadn't opened yet, but the prep crew was there with Bob. Blake scowled at her and hissed, "Not a word!"

Kara nodded and pursed her lips.

They found Bob setting up glasses behind the bar. He almost dropped one when he saw Blake and Kara walking toward him.

"Is Harold all right?" Bob asked nervously.

Blake placed his hand on the counter. "Harold is just fine."

Bob looked from Blake to Kara. Her heart ached at the worry on his old face.

"Bob, you have a Nagant revolver you brought home from Korea, don't you? Just like Harold's, but without the star, right?" Blake was all business.

Bob glanced under the counter where he kept the gun.

"Can I see it?"

Bob was silent.

"You know I can get a warrant to search the place."

Kara was looking at Blake. She wanted to soften the blow. Bob looked downright scared.

He started to reach under the counter when Blake put his hand on Bob's shoulder and said, "Let me get it,

Souvenirs

Bob."

A couple of Bob's sons had noticed them and came over. Blake stood behind the bar, leaving Kara on the other side. She moved to block the men from interfering.

"Dad, what's going on?"

They tried to push past Kara. Arms crossed and face blank, she was as immovable as a stone wall.

Bob held up a hand and said, "It's okay, boys. He just wants to see my gun."

Using an ink pen, Blake lifted the unlocked lid of the ordnance box to find the gun at the bottom.

"Bob, do you keep this unlocked?"

"Why?"

Blake looked in the ordnance box and saw the container of rounds beside the gun. He looked up and saw that Bob's boys were blocked by Kara. Suppressing a smile, he noted that true to her promise, she hadn't said a word to anyone. Blake was impressed.

"Bob, can I take this with me?"

Bob looked confused. Blake said, "Bob, the bullet that killed Hollis Meyers was from this type of gun. That's why it looked so bad for Harold at first because of his Nagant and his ill-considered confession. He thought he was protecting you, didn't he?"

Kara turned her head and looked at Bob. It was breaking her heart to see him like this.

Blake said, "Bob, can I take this with me?"

"Yeah, sure. Sure. It's okay, boys. Harold didn't need to protect me. I didn't do anything."

Wrapping one of the bar towels around the ordnance box, Blake picked it up. "I'll take good care of it,

Chapter 30

Bob. I know this old gun has some memories attached to it."

Bob nodded; his eyes locked with Kara's. She returned his nod. "Kara, Harold asked me to keep my mouth shut."

Kara walked around to face Bob, tears pooling in his eyes. "Bob, I know." She pulled him close, "I know."

Bob wiped his face. "Blake, are you going to arrest me?" Bob's sons moved in.

Blake said, "For what? For having this old gun? Or being an old coot who's devoted to Harold? I'd have to arrest most of the town. No, Bob, I'm not arresting you today. If you had mentioned this a few days ago, it would have saved a lot of heartache."

Bob started to answer when Blake held up his hand. "I know, I know, Harold asked you to keep your mouth shut."

When Blake dropped Kara off at the diner, he said, "When I get to be old, I hope I have a friend like that."

Kara smiled and said, "Blake, I don't think you have to worry." She paused. "You will let me know what they find, right?"

"Right." He waited for her to walk into the diner before he pulled away. She didn't back down. She was more like Harold than he realized. Good thing she doesn't look anything like him, he thought. She had kept her promise to him and hadn't said anything or interfered in any way. She hadn't allowed anyone else to interfere either.

Chapter 31

Harold was at the diner when she arrived.

"Pops, why didn't you say anything about Bob's gun?" Kara asked.

Harold's face hardened. "What have you done to Bob?" he barked.

"Nothing. Blake went to get his gun. We didn't do anything but take his gun so it could be examined."

Harold left his coffee sitting on the counter and stalked out of the diner.

"Kara, what just happened?" Geneva asked.

"Mom, did you remember Bob has one of those Korean guns like Pops?"

Geneva's eyes widened.

"That's right. He does."

"I didn't remember until a few hours ago. Blake and I went to The Blue Gill. Bob gave his gun to Blake. Now Pops isn't happy with me."

"He thought Bob killed Hollis. That explains everything."

Kara nodded. "Pops is going to be pretty mad at me and Blake for a while."

"Kara, you're the light of his life. He can't stay angry

Chapter 31

with you for long. Don't worry, baby; it will be okay. I, on the other hand, can hold a grudge for a long time. I'll have words with Pops about this later." Geneva raised an eyebrow as she glanced toward the seat he had vacated.

"What I don't understand is how Harold could believe Bob killed Hollis. Bob is an ornery old coot, but he's harmless," Geneva said.

"I don't know either, Mom. I'm just glad it gets Pops off the hook for the murder. I just hope Bob doesn't get arrested."

Geneva's eyes softened. "Kara, they are a couple of old peas in a pod. Neither one could have murdered anyone. It would have been more in character for both of them to spend days enjoying the battle rather than killing off their source of fun. Harming someone just doesn't fit. Can you imagine either of them coming to blows with someone?"

Kara smiled. It was silly to imagine Pops and Bob trying to even wrestle anyone. Geneva patted her on the shoulder and walked away.

Kara began wiping tables and refilling napkin dispensers as she thought, Something about the murder is off-center. I just can't put my finger on it. The guilty one has to be someone who knows about the guns. Kara paused as she let the thought develop further. That would limit the number of people to the population of Monroe. The family had forgotten about Bob's gun; even Mom had forgotten about it. At least now I know why Pops confessed. He was protecting the people he loved.

Puzzled, Kara went about cleaning tables and serving people mechanically, full of questions without answers.

Souvenirs

Mike walked into the diner as Kara was making rounds with the coffee pot. Still lost in thought, she made her way over to the counter.

"Here for another free cup of coffee, Mr. Olson?" she asked.

"I heard Harold's out of jail. Congratulations! He and I had our differences in the past, but I'm not a twelve-year-old any longer. I hope I can get him to change his mind about me."

Kara smiled as she poured him a cup of coffee.

"I know he has good reason to doubt me," he continued, his hand over his heart. "I just want to show him I'm a responsible adult now. I promise never to borrow his rowboat. However, I can't promise not to court his beautiful granddaughter."

Kara laughed.

Mike took her hand. "I love hearing you laugh. Why, Miss Dyer, I think you're blushing!"

"I'll get you a menu."

"I'm not going anywhere right now, Beautiful."

Kara returned with the menu still smiling and blushing. "I need to see to some of the other customers for a moment. I'll be right back to get your order."

"For you, my dear, I will wait."

Kara circled the dining room, clearing tables and checking in with her customers before returning to Mike. She wanted to take time to sit with him and made sure there were no distractions, at least for a few minutes.

"So who is this Wes guy? He isn't competition, is he?" Mike asked when Kara finally sat down beside him.

"Wes? No. He's almost Mom's age."

Chapter 31

"Ah, so no other suitors I need to do battle with?"

Kara thought about Gabe. He was still overseas with the Marines. He never was a suitor because of the military restrictions on relationships. Besides, the chaplain in Germany had told her long-distance relationships could be extremely challenging. She thought again about her scars, realizing she wasn't willing to talk with Mike about them.

"No, not unless you think Stan's a suitor."

Mike's eyes narrowed. "Stan?"

Kara grinned at Mike. "No. No suitors."

A smile played around Mike's eyes. "I don't think he'd be a problem for me anyway."

Mike studied the menu for a moment. "I heard that handyman was injured while he was out fishing. Is he okay?"

"Randy? No, he isn't okay."

"He's still alive though, isn't he? Word is my warrior princess saved him." Mike looked up at her. "He hit his head or something?"

"He was hit on the head by someone, is more likely. I found him alive, but unconscious. We don't know what happened yet, but we'll find out."

"Ah. He seemed to be a jack-of-all-trades kind of guy. Delivered papers, fixed lawnmowers, and apparently likes to go fishing."

Kara remembered finding Randy in his boat, his face covered with flies. Her anger was fueled by the memory and Mike's attitude pushed her over the edge, causing her temper to flare.

She glared at Mike as she thought about freshening up his coffee, "accidently" spilling the hot liquid all over his lap. She took a deep breath and said, "Randy is a nice guy and super- smart when it comes to mechanical things. Everyone loves him."

"Sure they do, but he's just the paper boy," Mike quipped.

She had heard other insensitive comments from people all day and had even encouraged the exchange. She asked herself why Mike's words were getting under her skin. *I'm just tired, that's all,* she thought, willing herself to calm down. *Didn't I want to get people talking about the murder, Randy, and Pops' confession?* She managed to keep smiling and said, "You want to order something or are you just here for free coffee?"

"I'm here for the excellent coffee, and any other sinful delights you're offering."

Kara kept smiling and handed him the dessert menu. Mike pouted as he took it from her. "Not quite what I was thinking about."

Kara walked away as she said, "I'll be back in a minute to get your order. I need to check on my other customers."

When Kara returned to Mike he had decided on the lemon meringue pie. Kara returned to the kitchen to get it from the refrigerator. She banged the door closed and took a deep breath before walking back to the counter. Still smiling, she offered Mike the pie.

"Service with a smile; what more could a man want from a woman?" Geneva was standing near and put herself between Kara and Mike. "Please excuse me." She leaned over to check the napkin dispenser. "I was right; we're running out of napkins here. Let me just refill this. Kara, the

Chapter 31

Malie's just walked in. Could you get a booster seat for little Nancy?"

Kara's flashing eyes met her mother's. Without breaking her steady stream of words, Geneva added, "The booster seats are right over there. Nancy likes the one with the ladybugs on it."

Why was her mother telling her where the booster seats were? She knew where they were. She also knew Nancy liked the ladybugs. Now she was in the middle of a simple conversation with Mike and it wasn't going well. Kara suddenly looked up at Geneva. Oh, yeah, she thought. Mom's doing the 'mom thing' again. Kara smiled at Mike. She whispered "Thank you" to her mother as she walked by.

Kara managed to keep busy and not talk to Mike again. He seemed oblivious to how upset she had gotten with him and had moved down the counter with his pie to chat with other customers.

Souvenirs

Chapter 32

Kara's thoughts were all jumbled by the time she went for her usual afternoon swim. The doctors had said to exercise to keep the scar tissue flexible. The good thing was she never considered swimming to be an exercise. When she was in the water, she just felt free.

Moving through the water, her short choppy strokes reflected her anger. She swam with sudden thrashing turns. She dove again and again frightening away the sunfish as she erupted out of the water. Kara kept dwelling on the fact that the answers were at the tip of her tongue. However, for now, not much made sense. Exhausted, she floated back to the dock and toweled off before going inside.

When she reached her room, she opened a dresser drawer, spilling items all over the floor. Running her hands through her hair, she squatted to pick everything up. Letters from Gabe were scattered amongst socks and bracelets. Brow wrinkled, Kara picked them up, sorting the unopened out-of-sequence ones. Reluctantly, she sat them aside and reread the others.

A peace that even her swim was not able to invoke enveloped her. She stood staring out the window for a few moments before folding the letters back into their envelopes and placing them on the dresser. She pulled off her swim suit and looked in the mirror at her scars. Her breasts were intact, though she couldn't imagine how they had been missed. Her bullet proof vest had taken a couple of hits and she recalled the sound of a few of the ceramic tiles cracking. When the shrapnel pierced through the ceramic shielding, ripping open her side, the gas had ignited, burning her from her hip to just under her neckline. She remembered thinking, This is what it's like to die.

Now, standing in her bedroom in Indiana with the sparkling lake just outside her window, she let herself relive the awful memories. She remembered a red haze, and how she had looked up, expecting to see the insurgents moving in to kill the remaining wounded. Instead, she found herself gazing into Gabe's gray eyes, which were filled with worry. She thought it was odd that he had taken off his sunglasses, as he always wore them. The marine squad had been returning from a patrol when they came across the ambushed convoy. She had gotten to know those guys pretty well over the past several months and this time they hadn't called her "Dyer" when they found her. They had called her "Kara".

Gabe had stayed with her until the medics had taken her away. Later when he came to see her before they sent her to the hospital in Germany, he had called her a hero. He told her the guys were all impressed she didn't quit after everyone higher ranking than her had been killed. He said lives had been saved because she had pulled the wounded into a protected area. He said she had been strong.

What was going on with her now? She looked at her scars, the ugly lines across her stomach and the puckered waxy areas along her left side. Her fingertips brushed against the letters on the dresser. The letters were written by a hero who had treated her as an equal. Walking over to her desk, she opened her photo album and looked at the pictures of herself with the squad. She laughed. She was never considered small but when she was beside those Marines, she looked like a munchkin. The thing is they had never treated her as small.

Kara had an enemy to fight back then. Being the object of highest resistance had made the enemy come to her. There was still an enemy to fight now, and he was hiding in plain sight. She would have to make the killer come to her, but this time it would be on her terms.

She pulled on a pair of cut-offs and an old t-shirt before writing an e-mail to Gabe.

"Things have gotten complicated around here. I don't even know where to start. A developer came into town and wanted to buy some land from Pops. Of course, Pops wasn't having any of it, but the developer was determined and got Pops to listen to him. Pops seemed to be considering the idea when this developer was killed a few days later with a Nagant, the same gun Pops brought back from Korea. The thing is it wasn't his Nagant that killed the guy. Pops confessed because he thought his buddy, who also has a Nagant, might have killed the developer. Eventually, the police figured out it wasn't Pops' gun. I don't know what will happen to Pops' friend. Our lawyer is working on getting Pops out of the trouble he's still in for interfering with a police investigation. For the life of me, I can't believe anyone in Monroe would have killed this guy. Most folks in Monroe didn't even know he was here, and if you weren't a

Chapter 32

local, there is no way you would know about the Nagants.

"Randy, one of the locals, was attacked and hit in the head while fishing and he's still in a coma. It might be related, I don't know. I can't imagine fishing has become competitive enough around here to try to kill someone, and honestly, everyone in town loves this guy. He doesn't come off as being very smart at first, but he's actually some kind of genius with engines and mechanical things. I went looking for him because I wanted to talk with him about the guy he saw walking down the road. From what I can piece together, I think he might have passed the murderer before dawn the morning the developer was murdered. When Randy didn't show up for work, his boss seemed to think he had gone fishing. There had been a storm the night before, making for great fishing conditions. I found Randy, unconscious in his boat with his head busted open. Doc Marr said he would have been dead if I hadn't found him.

"I want to beat senseless whoever tried to kill Randy. Who in Monroe would want to harm him? I think whoever hurt him is the killer we're looking for.

"Other exciting news: We had a tornado the other night. We're alright, but one farm lost everything—animals, as well as buildings.

"I had a date with a guy I've known since I was a kid, but it didn't go so well. He still seems interested, though. I was nervous the whole time and the entire evening was pretty uncomfortable. I didn't think I would see him again, but he's come to the diner and flirted with me. I guess I'm just not ready yet.

"I was glad to receive your letter, and you're right, I do feel safer when I can see or reach my gun. Mom would be mad if she knew I kept it loaded and under my pillow at night.

I do miss you guys and wish I could see you all again.

"As always, Kara"

She re-read the e-mail. It was so simple when she wrote it down. Everything made more sense to her. She realized she had been making things a whole lot more difficult than they needed to be. It felt good to be able to write to Gabe.

She hit the send button then took out a piece of paper and started a list.

At the top of the page she wrote, "Things I Know"

Her pen hovered over the sheet, her eyes growing distant as she looked, unseeing, out the window. Finally, she began writing.

1. Hollis is killed with a Nagant.
2. Pops confesses to protect Bob.
3. Randy passes someone he thought was Mitch, but wasn't.
4. Shots were heard on the island.
5. Pops' gun wasn't fired.
6. Randy was attacked.

Things I Need to Find Out

Who killed Hollis?

Why?

Who attacked Randy?

Was the person Randy saw, the one who attacked him?

Did Randy ever know it wasn't Mitch on the road?

Why was Randy attacked?

Chapter 32

Who knew Pops and Bob each had a Nagant?

Who is familiar with the ordnance used for that weapon?

She tacked the list to the corkboard above her desk, thinking she would add to it later. For now, she was able to let go of it and focus on other things, like how hungry she was.

Souvenirs

Chapter 33

Kara's mind was working overtime; the answers were right there in front of her. It seemed the more she tried to catch them, the more out of focus the images became. It was like an itch she just wasn't able to scratch. Why Randy? she wondered. For that matter, why Hollis? She knew she needed to protect Mitch, but wasn't sure from whom.

The diner stayed busy for the next couple of days and Kara was grateful she was too tired to think. Bob had joined Harold for breakfast this morning, and it was almost as though nothing had happened. It was good to see the old guys putting in their two cents about the new biology teacher at the high school, resumes from prospective deputies and Indiana University's football chances.

Kara fretted that she still hadn't heard back from Blake about Bob's gun. At home in her room, she stared at the list she had posted. Someone had been walking on the road the night Hollis was murdered. Randy thought he had passed Mitch. That person had to be the murderer. Why attack Randy? she thought as she thumped her desk. As far as Kara could tell, Randy didn't even know the person he had seen walking down the road wasn't Mitch. Randy was no threat to the murderer.

Chapter 33

Kara realized he must have seen something else. Had the killer known it was Randy who passed him? Who could miss that old beat-up, six-cylinder Nova? That Nova is almost as infamous as Pop's pickup truck.

She continued to be transfixed by the list. Had Randy seen something else? He must have. The killer would have to do him in then. In Kara's mind, she pictured the murderer had been in a hurry for some reason to not have finished the job. Something had caused him to risk leaving Randy alive.

Frustrated, she turned away from the list and went to her computer to check her e-mail. She was glad to see a message from Gabe.

"Dyer, stop dating losers. It seems pretty obvious there are plenty of them in Monroe. Why else would your date's failure make you feel like it's your fault? Stop thinking it's your fault when things aren't working with other people. I'm not unhappy about the fact you thought things didn't go well with that guy. I can't believe your mom is letting you date losers anyway.

"Please be careful and don't put your nose in anything dangerous. Murder is serious stuff. However, because I know you will keep poking at it, you need to broaden your search. There may be others who aren't necessarily locals who knew about the guns. You said the population of Monroe nearly doubles with all the summer residents.

"From what you've told me, your granddad is a tough old bird. I imagine his buddy is as well. They both survived Korea, after all. Things will work out okay, you'll see.

Souvenirs

"I know this isn't how we ought to be having this conversation. It should be taking place on that island you're always talking about. Please don't get too involved with anyone until I have a chance. I'm not asking you to stop seeing all those losers. Well, maybe I am. I know it's asking a lot. I also know I didn't tell you this to your face when I had the opportunity. I'm such a coward. I've come to realize I miss your laugh. I miss that awesome hair of yours. I miss you more and more each day. Save some room for me, please, and stop chatting up that real estate guy."

Kara realized she had stopped breathing. The text blurred on the screen as she brushed tears from her eyes. "Coward?" she thought. Gabe was one of the bravest people she had ever known. She turned to the dresser and looked at the small stack of letters he had written. She cherished each and every one of them. She was Army enlisted and he was a Marine officer, a major road block to any relationship they might have had. Her head was spinning as her hands hovered over the keyboard, searching for how to respond.

She hit reply and paused.

"I talked to the Chaplin before I left about long-distance relationships and he said they were not easy to maintain. Yes, I will save room for you, as much as you need. The island will always be here, and so will I, ready for conversations."

She re-read Gabe's note, realizing he thought she was dating Stan. She reached for his unopened letters, her smile fading. They were out of order and she needed to wait until the next one in line showed up. She hoped the mail trucks carrying the missing letter had made it through instead of being targeted by the insurgents.

Chapter 33

That afternoon she swam strong, even strokes southward along the shore-line. The scars on her side pulled, but she continued making progress in spite of her discomfort. The lake was still as she reached the entrance to the inlet. As she turned back, she swam away from the shoreline to avoid the brambles protruding into the lake. Pausing, she saw the shoreline had become more distant than she had intended. While she wasn't tired, she knew she needed to stay closer to the shore. When she dived to execute her turn, a flash caught her eye. Curious, she dived down toward the object. It was a concrete boat anchor with a set of oars and a blanket tied to it. When she pulled at the blanket, a camera floated from the folds.

Randy's camera! She grabbed the camera and pulled at the blanket that was firmly attached to the anchor. Deciding she wouldn't be able to take the oars, she rose to the surface. She looked around to make sure she had good bearings before swimming as fast as she could to the house to call Blake.

Souvenirs

Chapter 34

The next morning Blake stopped in at the diner for coffee. He motioned for Kara to sit beside him.

"Okay. It was lucky you happened to be swimming out there. Most folks don't swim that far out," he said.

"Are you here to nag me for swimming too far? I don't often swim down that way either. I wasn't thinking and just happened to go that way. So, what's up?"

"The divers pulled up the boat anchor, oars, and a stadium jacket. Walt reported one of the concrete boat anchors he had been making grew legs and walked away a few days ago. The anchor looks like one of his. He thought some kid took it. That might be. However, I can't believe any kid in his right mind is going to get rid of a Bears stadium jacket. It looks like the real deal."

"A Bears jacket? It wasn't a blanket?" Kara asked.

"No. The most interesting thing was the underwater camera. Someone had tried to destroy it, but it was intact, thanks to the waterproof case. We sent it to the lab in Fort Wayne to see if there's anything on it."

Kara asked, "Have you heard anything about the gun yet?"

"No. I'm going to call the lab after a bit to check on

this new stuff. I'll ask about the gun then."

"What about Bob?"

Blake's hand flew up in the air. "Kara, Harold confessed. It doesn't matter that it was a lie to protect Bob. Why? Inquiring minds want to know. Cops do tend to have inquiring minds."

He stood up and started to walk away then stopped and turned. "That means they both interfered with a police investigation. People what to know if either of them knew something. There are some things Harold will still have to answer for, and now Bob has to convince police officers he isn't guilty."

Kara stood still and didn't say anything while Blake's eyes rolled toward the sky. "Kara, I'll see what I can do." He watched the smile begin to fill her face. "No promises here. They broke the law. Harold lied; Bob withheld evidence." He spun on his heels and left her standing there.

Kara watched Blake walk out, knowing he would do what he could. Pops had lied, and Bob hadn't come forward about his Nagant. This wasn't going to be easy.

When she saw her mother, she said casually, "I'm going to visit Randy this evening. You need anything while I'm out?"

After pleading with the nurses, Kara was allowed in to see Randy, who was attached to a ventilator. His color was greatly improved from when she had first found him that awful day on the lake. Kara pulled a chair up to his bed. It broke her heart that he was laying there so still, with the machines humming ominously.

She held his hand in hers. "Randy, I think we found the oar someone hit you with, and the black jacket the murderer was wearing when you saw him on the road that night." She watched his face for any indication he was hearing her. "That guy you passed on the road? It wasn't Mitch. Did he try to kill you because you saw something?" She frowned at the monitor and sighed as she brushed his hair off his forehead.

Kara continued, "There was this guy I knew when I was in the Army. He likes me. He doesn't want me to get too involved with anyone else. I like him and I've been bursting to tell someone." She looked at the door to make certain no one else could hear before she leaned toward Randy. "I reckon that right now you're pretty safe to tell my secrets to." She spent the next several minutes telling Randy about Gabe before a nurse came in to let her know visiting hours were about over. Kara patted his hand, kissing him on the forehead. "Later, Randy. Next time I'll bring in a book and read to you."

"You did a good job shutting down the grill today, Mitch." Wes said. "Geneva and I are going to do some buying for the diner and need to have a meeting with one of the suppliers. You want to ride along to learn something about the restaurant business?"

Mitch said, "Sure, let me check with my parents. I'm still grounded." His family had made arrangements to live in a used trailer while they rebuilt the farm, and until it was delivered, Mitch would continue to stay with the Dyer's.

"Ouch. Yeah, I forgot about that," Wes said. "Beer. Island. Busted. Who gave you that beer, anyway? None of you are old enough to buy it. Bob sure wouldn't have sold it to you," Kara remarked.

Mitch answered, "It was already there on the island,

Chapter 34

in a cooler."

Wes exclaimed, "Already there? You drank old beer?"

"No. There was still ice in the cooler and everything. It wasn't old."

Wes raised his eyebrows and tilted his head. "Cooler? Ice? And you're telling me one of your buddies didn't bring it? A local beer gnome? Maybe I should start visiting the island myself. Can't beat free beer."

Kara was curious. "Where did you find it?"

"Behind the cabin under that really big lilac bush there."

Wes said, "Lilac bush, huh?"

Kara knew the ancient lilac grove. It made the ultimate natural hide-out for kids. You could crawl between the mass of limbs and find a cozy little room made by the old lilacs. In the spring, it had the added benefit of smelling good.

Mitch said, "We figured someone had forgotten about it and it was finders-keepers."

Kara asked, "So why did you go home?"

Mitch said, "I got seriously sick then those gun shots sounded so close, I guess I got a little scared."

Kara was suddenly alert. "Mitch, what about the gun shots scared you?"

He paused before answering, looking guilty.

Kara cajoled, "It's alright. What about the gun shots scared you?"

Mitch looked at the floor. "Harold is kind of scary sometimes. When we heard the shots we thought he was shooting at us."

Souvenirs

Geneva laughed when Wes said, "Harold is kind of scary to me, too sometimes."

Kara coaxed Mitch along. "So, you thought someone was shooting at you?"

"Yeah, it was only a couple of shots and then it stopped, but I was already spooked. I'd been hearing noises since we got there, like in one of those zombie movies. We found the beer later and I drank my fair share then I got sick. It was scary when the shots went off. It wasn't that fun and I was kind of ready to leave anyway. So I did."

Kara asked, "Do you remember the time you heard the shots?"

Mitch shook his head. "No, it was the middle of the night. I left right after that."

Where did the beer come from? Kara wondered.

Chapter 35

She locked up the diner and walked to The Blue Gill, passing Mike's car parked on the street. She hadn't seen Mike for a day or two, and after the way he had talked about Randy, she didn't want to.

When Kara was a teenager, her parents had kept her from dating Mike. The funny thing was she hadn't actually been disappointed at the time. Now she was starting to realize even then she had known he wasn't a good guy.

He's different than I am, Kara thought as she looked down the street at the canopy of trees shading the sidewalks. We come from different places and have different life experiences. She rubbed the scars running across her ribcage.

The Blue Gill wasn't open yet, but she knew Bob was already there, along with Pops. Kara's brow wrinkled when she saw the cruiser parked out back. She paused at the back door and straightened her shoulders before opening it and walking in.

"Kara, what do you want now?" One of Bob's sons snapped. "Every time you come in here you bring trouble."

"I need to talk to Pops. Is he here?"

The man grunted, stepping aside to let her pass.

Souvenirs

Bob was stacking glasses behind the counter and Pops and Blake were sitting on bar stools.

"Just the people I want to talk to," Kara said.

Bob's eyes narrowed as he turned his back on her.

Blake's head sagged when he heard Kara's voice. His eyes issued her a warning as she approached the bar.

Bob continued to keep his back to Kara. The chill coming from him was saving the place a ton of money on the air conditioning bill.

Kara started, "Bob, I know you're mad at me."

"Mad? What in the world would make you think I was mad at you?" Bob said without turning around.

Kara caught the movement of one of the boys walking toward her. She said, "Bob, I don't think you did it. I don't know how both of you thought the other one did. Aren't you guys friends?"

Harold said, "I didn't think Bob killed anyone. It was just he had the only other gun."

Bob looked up at his son, who paused before going back to the storage room. "My boys aren't happy with you."

"I wouldn't be happy with me either if the situation were reversed. Bob, you know something you're not remembering. I guess that's what Blake and Pops are here for. Am I right?"

Blake grunted.

"Remember what?"

"I don't know. Mitch told me the beer was already on the island. His buddies didn't bring it. He hadn't mentioned it before because it didn't seem that relevant to him, but it is. He also mentioned they heard the gun shots right around the time Hollis was killed."

Chapter 35

"I wasn't anywhere near the crime. I was here. I locked up and then went home."

Blake said, "But you didn't go straight home. You had a flat. You weren't happy about it either."

Bob's eyes widened, "Oh, right. I did. That's right. I meant to have Vern change that tire before it went flat."

Blake said, "Why didn't your boys lock up for you?"

Bob smiled, "Oh, you know. They have families to go home to. I remember how that is."

Blake said, "They went home early?"

"No, they left at the regular time. I stayed late. There was a guy here who stayed until after we closed. He had too much to drink. As a matter of fact, I took his keys away and settled him into his car to sleep it off."

"A guy? Who?"

"Oh, I forget his name -- that Olsen kid. That young man Kara was here with the other night."

Kara's head shot up. "Mike?"

Bob nodded, "Yeah. He has a real nice car."

Blake looked at Kara. "He was drunk? Here at The Blue Gill?"

Kara's head was spinning. "Are you certain it was Mike?"

Bob impatiently tossed the towel he was holding onto the bar.

"I just said I didn't catch his name," Bob snapped. "But you can't miss that fancy red car of his."

Kara made a low grunting noise as Blake turned to her. Her dark eyes became distant as he regarded her before turning reluctantly back to Bob.

Blake asked, "After you put him in his car, then

what?"

"Oh, that was all kinds of fun. He tried to help himself to one last drink and ended up falling down behind the bar. I had to go around and help him up. All but dragged him to the parking lot. He dropped like a rock as soon as I let go of him. I didn't think I'd ever get him in his car. Then I had that flat on the way home. I'm just getting too old for this."

It confounded Kara that a control freak like Mike would allow himself to get drunk. So drunk, in fact, he wasn't in charge of the situation. A snob like Mike wouldn't get drunk at a dive like The Blue Gill in the first place. She shook her head and looked at Harold, who said, "I never did like that kid."

Blake winked at Kara. "Yeah, like that's something we don't know."

Bob sighed, looking at Harold before facing Kara. "It takes a lot for Harold to dislike someone. You need to pay attention, Kara."

Kara hugged her grandfather and said, "Yeah, I'm kind of learning the hard way."

She noticed the pained expression on Bob's face, knowing full-well this gentle old man could not have harmed anyone.

Blake said, "Stop or someone will have to hug me." He looked at Bob and Harold. "I sure don't want to be hugged by you old guys."

Bob's eyes twinkled.

"Bob, can you remember any more? Did you see anything on the way home?" Blake asked.

"Just you, Blake. It was pretty late. Next morning

Chapter 35

I came back and that young man was sitting on the steps waiting for me because I had his keys."

Blake said, "That must have been before they found the body."

Bob nodded his head.

Harold said, "I can add 'drunk' to the list of items I don't like about that guy. It's unfortunate he's moved down here. I honestly didn't think a pretty boy like him ever would show up back here, but now we have to deal with him. Stan is disturbing enough." Harold's face wrinkled up in a grimace, making Bob laugh.

Kara left The Blue Gill, with that unsettled feeling in the back of her mind. There were questions she had wanted to ask Blake, but she didn't because he had given her a strange look when she walked in. Bob didn't know anything. It surprised her that Mike would allow himself to get drunk like that, at The Blue Gill, no less. She shook her head. I need to stay away from him and wait for Gabe, she thought.

As she walked back to the diner, she noticed Mike's car was gone and Blake was parked around back beside her car. She leaned in. "Well?"

"Well, yourself."

"You first. I have to say, being an informer is kind of fun." Kara said.

Blake just smiled.

"Out with it." Kara demanded.

Blake relented, counting off on his fingers. "Okay, Bob's gun was fired, but there aren't any prints on anything, including the locker. Bob's prints should have been all over it. Harold's gun is clean, which I expected. The markings on the bullets from Bob's gun are the same as the one that killed Hollis. The hair on the oar is Randy's. If the oar had prints they washed away, and the anchor is one that was stolen from Walt. The jacket is a Chicago Bears stadium coat with gun powder residue all over it."

Kara's mouth opened and didn't close.

Blake said, "Your turn."

Kara just stared at Blake.

Blake opened the door and stepped out of the car. "I said your turn. Kara, stop looking at me like I'm speaking Greek. What do you have?"

"Nothing close to that and you've already heard it. Mitch says the kids didn't bring the beer with them. He said they found it on the island in a cooler with ice. As far as I can tell Bob doesn't know anything, but Pops is certain he does. Mitch also says he was spooked even before they found the beer or heard the shots. He thought he heard zombies on the island."

"Beer and zombies on the island, huh? Except for the zombies, I agree with you; my information is better. It's a little odd the beer was already there, in a cooler with ice. I bet if we question the kids we'll find out one of them put it there."

Kara said, "I think those kids are telling the truth. Someone was shooting a gun that the kids on the island could hear. Why would they all keep lying about the beer after they have been caught? One of them would have told the truth by now. It's kind of creepy to think that someone has been drinking beer on Indian Island, and it may be related to the murder."

Blake nodded. "I figured the kids were telling the truth when the gun came back clean. Bob's prints should

<h1 style="text-align:center">Chapter 35</h1>

have been all over the gun, and the ammo box. Everything was obviously wiped clean."

Kara said, "It does look like the murder was premeditated. It was someone who knew Pops and Bob had the same kind of gun, someone who knew Pops had a fight with Hollis, and that could be anyone in Monroe."

Blake said, "Even your Mom didn't remember Bob had one of those guns."

Kara said, "But Pops did."

Blake turned his head away. "Yep, he did." He slapped the top of the car. "Kara, Harold is making me crazy. Now I've got to deal with this."

"Blake, do you suspect Bob?"

Blake's mouth was set in a hard line, the anguish evident in his eyes as he looked at Kara. He stooped down and started picking up stones. "No, I don't. The facts are Bob owns the murder weapon and we have that stupid confession. Anyone would think Harold is trying to cover for Bob. He's just not helping the situation any."

Blake stood up and threw stones one at a time at the dumpster. "Meanwhile there's someone who knew about the existence of both guns. They also knew what ordnance to use. You can't just put any kind of round in one of those, and there's the easily identifiable coat with ordnance residue on it. That coat was found tied to a stolen anchor and wrapped around an oar with Randy's hair on it."

Kara had forgotten about the black coat. "Wait! Randy said something about how the person he passed on the road had on a hooded black jacket. Mitch could never afford a stadium jacket." Frowning, she added, "His dad is a Colts fan and wouldn't buy him Bears gear. Mitch also told me if he had actually seen Randy he would have accepted a ride home."

"Yeah, just what I was thinking. It looks like Randy did see the murderer."

Kara remembered her conversation with Beth. "No one knew where Randy was that morning. Beth just made a guess that he had gone fishing, so how could someone know where he was?"

"Good question. Randy's in a coma, but still alive. That must concern the killer a little bit."

Kara's chest tightened and she grabbed Blake's arm in mid-throw. She hadn't considered someone might still be trying to kill Randy. "Could someone get to Randy even though he's in the hospital?"

Struck by the concern in her voice, Blake studied her face. "He's protected. No one is going to get to him who isn't on the visitors' list. You're not even on that list."

Kara cried out, "But Blake, I got in last night! I spent almost a half hour talking to him before they threw me out."

Chapter 36

Blake was already in his cruiser making a call to put some guards on Randy. Kara paced until he got back out of the car.

Blake rubbed his forehead. "Randy's okay. The security guards at the hospital will keep an eye on him until an officer arrives. The nurses aren't going to let anyone in at all unless accompanied by an officer."

Kara sank down, sitting on her heels and rubbing her face tiredly.

Blake squatted down beside her. "Well, we aren't any closer to knowing who the murderer is."

Kara whispered, "But Randy knows."

Blake threw a sharp glance at Kara before continuing to lob stones across the lot. "Harold has made it look like either he's an accomplice to Bob, or the other way around. At least we know where Harold was when Randy was attacked." Blake stood up and threw the last stone with the velocity of a fastball, complete with the leg kick.

Kara drove back to the house turning over all the information in her head. The answer had to be someplace in there.

Okay, Kara, she thought. What do you know? I

Souvenirs

know Bob's gun fired the bullet that killed Hollis.

She sighed as she thought, That's almost as bad as Pops' confession. Her nose wrinkled. Even Pops thinks Bob knows something. She pushed the hair away from her eyes. "Pops knows Bob better than almost anyone," she said out loud.

Kara glanced at the empty seat beside her. "Someone left enough beer in a cooler on the island to get those kids drunk. Who would do that? Who else has been out on the island?" The sound of the tires pulling the hot tar off the road kept pace with her thoughts as she wiped the sweat from her forehead and glanced in the rearview mirror, continuing to talk to herself.

"When did Bob's gun get taken? When did it get returned?" Kara thumped the steering wheel. "Did Mike see something while he was supposed to be sleeping it off in his car?" She frowned at the field of sunflowers. "How did the attacker know where Randy was fishing? Why would anyone who knew Randy want to hurt him?" Nothing connected. Drawing in a deep breath she shook her head. Blake must be pulling his hair out. She was glad she wasn't a cop.

Kara down-shifted, realizing all the information she knew so far didn't tell her anything; it only created more questions. Her mouth set in a strained line, she looked at her reflection in the rearview mirror. Again she spoke aloud. "Why kill Hollis? Why would anyone in Monroe want to kill him? Who knew about the guns?"

She snorted. "Just about everyone, but when it comes to guns, most folks around here think about .22s or shotguns, not old war trophies."

Chapter 36

Pops had needlessly placed himself in danger then ended up in jail. Now it appeared Bob was headed that way. Her eyes hardened as she glared into the rearview mirror. "At least Bob will be safe in jail if he does know something." She shook her head. "Randy's still in danger though." She laughed suddenly, remembering the conversation with Mitch. "And then there are the zombies Mitch heard on the island." She suddenly sobered. "And now Mitch is in danger."

The fields of golden sunflowers, tasseled aromatic corn, and soybeans blurred past. The air was filled with the earthy scents of summer. Kara whipped the car off the road and pulled to a stop, resting her head briefly on the steering wheel before leaning back to stretch her neck. She opened the car door and walked to the field of sunflowers that lifted their heads to the sky. Sitting in the grass with her head in her hands, she suddenly cried. "Enough! This is just giving me a headache!" She stood and walked back to the old Ford, trying several times to start it before the engine wheezed and finally turned over. She pulled back onto the road, heading for home.

Chapter 37

Geneva smiled at Beth as she sat at the counter. "What will you have today?"

"How's the tuna melt?"

Geneva grinned, "Great, as always. One tuna melt with the works?"

"Yeah, sounds good." Beth looked around the dining room. "Things seem to have settled down in here a bit."

Geneva surveyed the diner and laughed. "Things have gotten back to a more normal pace. The interest in the affairs of the Dyer family has finally waned. Our lawyer, with Blake's help, convinced the D.A. they didn't want to prosecute Harold, and so far, they haven't arrested Bob."

Geneva was interrupted by the sound of a pan dropping on the floor, followed by a curse from Mitch. Wes's laughter broke the stunned silence for a moment. Geneva smiled at Beth. "It may not be all that calm after all."

She continued, "Mitch has actually been working out well as an assistant cook. He's getting to be an expert on making eggs over-easy." Geneva paused to listen to Wes, who was still chuckling and saying, "The mop is over there, dish boy, where it always is."

Beth smiled. "Have you heard how it's going over

at his folk's place? I heard they were going to live in a used doublewide until the house is rebuilt."

Geneva nodded. "The Wilkes' are expecting delivery of the trailer in a day or two. The cement pad was poured last week and they're putting up one of those metal barns. I think they're working on the foundation for the new house this week. Once they start on actual construction of the house, I'm afraid we'll lose Mitch for at least a while."

"Are you thinking of hiring him permanently?"

"I certainly would like to. He's turning into a pretty good short-order cook. It's been a real help since it's been so crazy around here."

Geneva paused, looking around the kitchen. Wes was offering Mitch suggestions on how to use the mop. She sighed, "Something not so crazy would be a blessing at this point."

Beth leaned forward. "I hear Kara went on a date. How did that go?"

Geneva looked over her shoulder, making certain Kara wasn't within earshot, and whispered, "He's not the choice I would make for her."

Beth whispered, "Well, I thought he was rich. He sounds like a real catch to me."

Geneva rolled her eyes, "Money isn't everything. Character has a lot to do with it and he doesn't have a bit of shame. You should have heard him in here the other day flirting with Kara. I should have had Wes throw him out."

Beth's eyes widened, "Really?"

Geneva said, "Really," and took Beth's order to the kitchen.

When Geneva returned with her order, Beth said,

Souvenirs

"Well, he can't be as bad as Stan."

They both looked at each other and started laughing. Beth took a sip from her Coke and said, "You know, I haven't seen Stan around for a couple days."

Geneva shrugged. "Maybe he went out of town."

Beth speculated, "If he did, he didn't notify anyone. I was in the post office before coming here and they were complaining about how Stan's mail was backing up."

Kara had walked in the back door of the kitchen and heard the last bit of conversation. "What are you saying about Stan?"

Beth looked sheepish and said, "Only that he hasn't picked up his mail for several days. The postmaster was complaining."

Kara said, "Oh, he must just be out of town." Geneva nodded her head. "He said something about some big deal the other day, but it probably wasn't local. He did hint it was something he found by checking listings."

She fidgeted with the salt shaker. "Come to think of it, I haven't seen him in more than just several days. It's been since before the tornado. What did he say he was doing?"

Kara didn't have any warm fuzzy feelings toward Stan, but he was a fixture in the community. It wasn't like him to just disappear.

After the diner closed, she walked over to Stan's office. The building was scarcely larger than a shed, but well-maintained. The tiny lawn was mowed, but the flowers in the pots were wilting. Sticking her finger into a pot, she noticed the soil felt dry. "These things need watering," Kara murmured. Stepping up onto the front porch, she turned the door handle and found it locked.

She walked around to look in one of the windows that faced the street and saw that the computer was on and paper was falling on to the floor from the fax machine. She jiggled the window. Remembering her promise to Blake, Kara looked down the street toward the police station, an old brick bank building that had been repurposed. His cruiser was parked out front. She tried the window again before heading for the station.

"Blake, have you seen Stan?" Kara asked.

Incredulous, Blake dropped the paperwork he was holding. "Kara Dyer! Are you looking for Stan?"

Kara made a face at Blake. "Yes. I don't think I've seen him since the tornado. He's usually in the diner hitting on me at least twice a week."

"You know, I think you're right. He is in the diner hitting on you quite a bit. It's because you're such a tease."

"Blake, I'm serious."

"I am, too. Let's face it, you're female and available."

Kara rolled her eyes. "I'm worried."

Blake scrunched up his face. "I don't remember seeing him either, but then again he doesn't come looking for me. I'm not a single female." Blake didn't try to disguise his smile.

Kara crossed her arms. "Okay, you know I don't like him. To tell you the truth, if Beth hadn't been talking with my mom about not seeing him, I wouldn't have noticed. I know he's a slug, but he's our slug, and you know every town has to have one. If it's not him, it would just be someone else. It could be one of us!"

Blake sucked air in between his teeth. "When you put it like that, it makes it a little more urgent to solve this mystery. However, are you sure you want to be the one who finds him? He might interpret it the wrong way."

Kara narrowed her eyes and grunted.

Blake laughed.

Kara said, "He seems to have left everything on in his office."

Blake eyes widened. "Oh, I see. You've already been looking for him. Doing a little home invasion, are you? I think your actions are speaking louder than your words here. Sure that you're not just a little bit interested in Stan?"

"I'm sure. I just looked in his office window."

Blake nodded, "Yeah, I think Wes did tell me you're a Peeping Tom. Something about a bobble head fetish."

Kara's eyes narrowed even more.

Blake held up his hands and said, "Okay, okay. Let's go take a look, shall we? Then maybe you'll let me get back to some real police work."

Kara looked at Blake's computer monitor. "You're playing solitaire."

Blake laughed again. "Like I said, real police work."

They walked back to Stan's office and this time Blake peeked in the window. "Looks like that fax is working okay. There's a pile of paper on the floor in front of it. The answering machine is blinking, too. I can't see how many messages from here." Blake repositioned himself. "Looks like twelve messages. A real estate agent is going to check his phone messages even if he is away." Blake turned to Kara.

Someone shouted "Hey!" from the road.

Kara and Blake turned to the sound as Pops' old black pick-up truck turned into the parking lot.

Chapter 37

"What are you guys up to?" Pops asked.

"Looking for Stan."

"What in the world do you want with Stan?"

Blake shrugged. "He hasn't been around for a couple of days. Kara's worried."

She punched Blake in the arm.

Harold got out of the truck and peered through the window. "He sure left a mess if he went off on vacation. Stan is neat to a fault."

Blake eyes narrowed. "Yep." He looked through the window again and tried the door.

"I already did that," Kara said.

Blake's deadpan gaze met Kara's eyes. "Now I'm really worried about you."

"Fine, laugh all you want, but where is he?"

Blake pursed his lips. "I don't know. I'll ask around and see if anyone knows where he's gone to. I'd like to get in and take a look around before I do that though. Don't want to start any more rumors. We have enough of them going around already."

"Oh! There's a window open on the other side!" Kara was gone in a flash. Before Blake could catch up with her, she was already halfway through the window.

"Kara! No! Oh, okay. Don't touch anything; just open the door." Exasperated, Blake looked at Harold. "Does she ever stop?"

Harold raised his hands and shook his head. "No, and I don't think any of us really want her to."

Kara was standing in the open door waiting for Blake and Pops. "You can't be doing this stuff." He sighed. "You two stand here. If this turns out to be a missing person's case, I don't want this office compromised." Blake pointed back at Kara. "Stay!"

Pops craned his neck to see beyond the doorway. Blake pointed at him and said, "You too. Stay put."

Blake moved around the tiny office trying not to disturb anything, noting the open files on the desk and papers piled on the chair.

"I'm going to check his house and talk to his neighbors. You two go home."

"Blake, I want to help."

"No!"

"But --"

"I said, no. Stan's probably just on vacation. I seem to remember he goes to some real estate conference every year. He may be there. Could be anything. He doesn't have to notify the media if he just wants to get away for a few days, but this situation could -- and I repeat could -- be something more serious. Real police work." He glanced over at Harold. "Like I haven't had to do enough of that recently, no thanks to you and Bob. Let me follow up on this. I'll let you know what I find out. Okay?"

Harold looked down at the ground.

"Harold, take Kara and go home. Now."

Chapter 38

They found the plate of sandwiches Geneva had left in the kitchen for them. As they sat at the table eating, Harold said, "Why would Stan just leave?"

Kara put her sandwich down on her plate. "I don't know. He hinted he'd found a big real estate deal on the internet, but it just isn't like Stan to keep quiet about any big deal."

Harold asked, "Something he found on the internet?"

Kara looked up at Harold, "Yeah, he said most people don't look for real estate listings there."

Harold looked out the kitchen door toward the lake. "Really?"

Kara waited for Pops to continue. He appeared lost in thought. He hadn't finished his sandwich when Kara rose to go to bed. "Good-night, Pops," she whispered as she kissed him on the top of his head.

Still distracted, Harold reached up and patted her face. "Love you, Little Bit. Oh, tomorrow afternoon can you help me with using your computer?"

Kara was surprised. Pops had never liked computers. Her brow wrinkled at his sudden interest. "Sure, Pops, anytime." She regarded the back of his head. "Why?"

"You can find out about real estate listings on the computer, right?" he asked.

"Um, I think so. I haven't looked to buy property," she said. "Is this about Stan?"

"Uh-huh," he said, "Stan must have found something really interesting before he cleared town. I'd like to know what it is."

"Me, too. Good idea. I think we should check it out. Might give us another reason to tar and feather him."

Kara kissed him on the head again and left him staring out the back door at the darkness.

She went up to her room and checked her e-mail. Nothing from Gabe. She was concerned. She thought he had said he cared for her, that he wanted to take their friendship to a new level. She was all for it, but he hadn't replied to her acceptance of his offer. Maybe she read it wrong and scared him off. She reopened his last message and reread it. No. It seemed that is what he was saying.

No new messages from Gabe and the missing letter never arrived. She wondered if something had something happened to him? Her heart raced. Suppose he'd been wounded? She wouldn't be notified. Her gut hurt. She might lose him even before anything had a chance to start. He wasn't in a safe place now and she had already lost a few friends to the insurgents. She reread Gabe's e-mail, touching the screen as she did so. "Oh, Gabe, please be okay."

"Hey, Kara. How's the pecan buns this morning?" Blake settled himself at the counter.

"Gone. You should have been here earlier," Geneva said as she walked past, carrying an order to one of the

Chapter 38

tables.

Blake's face dropped into his best puppy-dog-eyed expression. He said to Kara, "Oh, well, I reckon a stack of pancakes will have to do."

"Well?" Kara hissed as she raised her eyebrows at him. "Have you found anything out about Stan yet?"

"Nope. It doesn't appear he planned on leaving. His newspapers are piling up at his house and the postmistress wasn't notified he'd be gone. It's all a little out of character for Stan. Might not be anything. People don't always bother to tell the post office or newspaper-delivery folks they're going to be out of town. But not Stan. He wants people to know he is a world traveler going to exotic places like Cleveland." Blake shook his head. "Not like Stan to sneak off. That's a little worrisome. The neighbors don't know anything either. Monroe has some of the snoopiest people around," Blake gave Kara a rueful smile. "We certainly don't have a need for an organized neighborhood watch."

Kara rubbed her forehead. "He's a conniving little whiner. However, this isn't like Stan. He's nothing if not a creature of habit. You could set your watch by him."

Blake nodded, "I have a missing person's report out. I found out he hasn't used his credit cards and I'm still waiting for more information from his bank. His car is gone. It looks odd, but he may have just gone crazy and left. Probably grief your constant rebuffs sent him over the edge."

Kara's eyes twinkled at Blake, "Well, I guess until we know more, the 'going crazy and leaving' explanation works best for him."

"What about my pancakes?"

Harold had come into the diner just before closing.

Souvenirs

He sat impatiently at the counter waiting for Kara to finish, holding some real estate flyers. His impatience had earned him a glare from Geneva.

"Pops, Kara's still working. Leave her be."

Harold just grunted and read the flyers again. When Kara took off her apron, Harold pounced. Shooting a glance at Geneva he said, "She's mine now!" Giggling, Kara allowed herself to be swept outside by her grandfather, who propelled her with a hand on her elbow. They had a brief argument over whether Kara would ride home in the truck or take the wagon home. He agreed to let Kara drive herself, but he followed her closely. She was able to grab a soft drink before being hustled upstairs to the computer.

"Okay, I want you to see if we can find out about any real estate sales in the area. I have these 'www' addresses here on these flyers." She turned to ask if Pops understood what a 'www' address was, but was met by a blank stare. He handed the flyers to Kara and she attempted to explain how to use search engines. He kept responding in a monotone "Uh-huh" to her explanations until she gave up. Turning to the keyboard, she typed in an address.

Kara glanced at Pops. "We're looking for any real estate stuff in the area, right?"

Harold nodded.

After about forty minutes, they hadn't discovered anything that would warrant Stan's enthusiasm.

Harold rubbed his head. "Well, that was a bust."

"No, wait. Let's look outside of our little area. Let's do a bigger search and include more than residential listings. Let's see if there are business listings." In a few seconds, they had several hits surrounding the Monroe

Chapter 38

area. They had already seen most of them in the previous search, but Kara narrowed it to higher-end listings, her eyes traveling down the screen. "What's this?"

Harold peered over Kara's shoulder at the screen and jumped as his eyes followed what she was pointing to.

He blurted, "Well, slap me and call me Betty! I was right!"

Harold put his hand on her shoulder. "Okay, what else? I can see it on your face. Cough it up."

"Pops, I don't know if it has any connection."

"But it's clearly on your mind. What is it?"

"It's Mike. I don't know what to make of him. He's doing things I didn't expect. He runs hot and cold. Nice one minute; mean the next."

Pops said, "And?"

"He's two different people. He was helping at the Wilkes farm, something I totally wouldn't expect from him. That was some pretty nasty work. I don't see Mike as a roll-up-your-sleeves kind of guy. Then he got roaring drunk at The Blue Gill. He's been a control freak since he was a kid. Why would he allow himself to get so drunk he couldn't drive home?"

Pops nodded. "Mikey always did like to ride roughshod over all the rest of you kids. Being in a condition where he wasn't in charge is not like him."

Kara agreed, "Right. It's even more remarkable he got drunk on beer in a bar that's way beneath his standards."

"Yep. I was real surprised he took you to The Blue Gill."

"I've been thinking it was my fault the date didn't go smoothly. Thinking back, he was the one who was distracted. Why would he still come on to me when he was only half-there?" She turned around in her chair to face Harold. "I wonder if there is any connection to Hollis?"

"Doesn't seem to be," Pops said. "This information," he continued, pointing at the screen, "is pretty shady. Hollis was planning a working family development that would actually improve the lake; affordable housing. He was trying to make contacts in the community. He wasn't trying to hide anything. Mike is trying to build a high-end resort and casino. He's been keeping real quite about it too." Pops crumpled the printout.

Harold had been watching Kara. He was plenty mad, but he still recognized the emotions playing over his granddaughter's face.

She turned to her grandfather. "Pops, let's go get him."

Harold put an arm around her shoulders and said, "That's my girl, but let's go find Blake instead."

Harold placed a call to Blake. Geneva insisted the two of them eat dinner before going off to stomp on Mike.

Wes had come home with Geneva, and Blake arrived just before the meal was served so Geneva shooed the Mitch and the rest of them to the dock while she finished up.

"Let me get this straight. A lake front resort here? Instead of houses he's putting in a hotel and casino?" Wes asked, incredulous.

"Yep, looks that way," Kara answered.

"But why keep it a secret?" Wes asked the others. Then he answered his own question. "Oh, yeah, you guys would stop him."

"Wes, the woods would be reduced by half and the

lake would die. Oh, I'm sure they would maintain it for hotel guests to use, but I bet they wouldn't bother to keep it healthy. The woods are essential to the health of the lake, but all the chemicals making their way to the lake from a development like that would destroy it, and eventually, the rest of the woods. It's an eco-system that's been in place longer than there has been an America. It's vulnerable; it needs to be protected," Kara said.

Harold nodded. "That's why you should finish your degree, so you can protect this lake."

"You can develop your own property. That isn't against the law, is it? I mean it is his," Wes said.

"Right, sort of," Blake said, "He does have to abide by the laws and some of those laws apply to land use. Monroe has some pretty tough regulations when it comes to the impact on the lake. The Association is quite effective in the development of those land-use laws." Blake pointed at Harold. "And in making certain they're enforced."

Wes nodded. "So now that you know all this, you're going to do some enforcing?"

Harold barked, "Dang right we are!"

Blake's eyebrows went up.

Harold continued, "The weasel almost got away with it. If he hasn't started anything, we'll be able to stop him. The damage could be really difficult to reverse if he's already got going on it."

Geneva walked out to the dock. "I'm not bringing dinner to you." With that pronouncement, they followed her up to the kitchen. Kara turned to smooth the printout down on the counter. She could have sworn her mother had patted Wes's backside.

Souvenirs

Blake said, "Stan must have found out about the development then approached Mike."

Kara added, "I'd like to approach Mike. I'd like to ask him about it in Braille."

Wes roared with laughter, "I'd pay to see that!"

Mitch puzzled, looking at the group as Blake pointed at Harold. "You will do no such thing. If I even think you two are going to do anything stupid, I'll put you under arrest. I'm not kidding!"

Kara started to say something, but Blake cut her off. "No, you're not taking the law into your own hands." He glared at Harold before turning back to Kara. "No, Kara. Just, no! You're much too angry with him right now. You'd be guilty of assault and battery. As far as I know, he hasn't done anything to break the law; you would be breaking the law. I don't want to arrest another member of your family."

Mitch listened intently.

Kara snarled as Harold and Geneva exchanged looks and Wes just stared at his plate.

"Developing his property is his business," Harold agreed. "He knows it isn't right because he's sneaking around to do it."

Wes said, "I don't know all the history here, but if what you're telling me about this Mike guy is true, and I believe it is," Wes glanced at Kara, "it might be something else."

Everyone had stopped eating and looked at Wes. "Think about it. He's not wanting to go up against you, Harold; he knows he would lose. He's always lost when he's gone up against you."

Geneva asked, "Why would he sneak around, if he is

at all, just because he's developing his property?"

"Good question," Blake interjected.

Geneva's brow wrinkled as she looked around the table. Sighing, she continued, "All evening you've been talking about horrible people and unpleasant occurrences. Can't we talk about something a bit lighter?"

They all looked at each other in the growing silence. Harold looked at Geneva with his most innocent expression and said, "No." They all burst out laughing.

Geneva, still laughing, said, "Well, rumor has it Stan left town because he realized since Mike is back, he could never win Kara."

Blake looked at Kara. "Really? Well, anyone who wins Kara's love is asking for a lot. Send them to me. I'll give them one of my flak jackets."

Kara batted her eyes. "What, sweet little me?"

Blake said, "Yeah, sweet little you who's going to stay away from Mike." He thought to himself, I wouldn't mind having you on my side in a fight, and I used to babysit you.

Harold cleared his throat. "Want to talk about something good? Let me tell you about Hollis Meyer's plan. Hollis had been developing property for years and built a reputation on the West Coast as someone who was always in balance with the environment. His goal was to develop communities that regular folks could afford, that were beautiful, and protected the natural eco-systems. Just looking at the septic designs shows that."

Harold looked at Kara. "I took the plans Hollis left with me to some experts I know and they were impressed. I checked on his reputation on the West Coast, too. It was excellent. He was a good guy all around. He could have made a lot more money than he did on the land he developed. He worked with Habitat for Humanity on each of his developments so a few families who couldn't afford to buy their own homes would have that opportunity. His developments always had restrictions on them so folks who purchased them couldn't resell them for more than a certain amount for upwards of fifty years. That way, he could keep them affordable for regular people. It's still a mystery to me why someone would want to kill him."

Blake nodded his head. "Yeah, he doesn't seem to have had any enemies."

Kara thought about the economy rental car he drove, the fact he wore old shoes and blue jeans. He was willing to humble himself to talk with Pops. He was a decent guy.

Harold slapped the table. "Hollis was divorced with joint custody for twin daughters. His ex-wife's company relocated her to a position in Fort Wayne and Hollis followed to stay close to his girls. Well, I've decided I'm going to move ahead with Hollis's plan and split the profits with his family."

Kara smiled at Pops as Geneva reached out and took Harold's hand in hers.

Wes said, "Well, that's great! I agree with Geneva. This is much too intense for me. Let's talk about something else. Geneva, where's the pie?"

Chapter 39

Kara pinned the Olson farm advertisement to the corkboard over her desk then restacked the letters from Gabe, turning the unread ones sideways. She thought about her date with Mike. She had been dazzled by all his charm and hadn't been able to see the ugliness going on behind his handsome looks and inviting smile. Mike had always used people, avoiding punishment by blaming others, hiding what he was doing because he didn't want to be stopped. He hadn't been honest about the development of the Olson farm for the same reason. He hadn't changed a bit.

Her memory became crystal clear. That day so long ago when they'd been stranded on the island was because he hadn't secured the rowboat. He hadn't gone for help. He took the only floatation device because he panicked. He snuck off when she wasn't looking. Later he said it didn't have enough air to support them both. He left her there, only trying to save himself. Her eyes narrowed as she recalled how he hadn't taken into account she was a swimmer. She had beaten him to the dock because she was so angry. He wasn't heading there anyway because he wasn't going to get help like he said later. He simply didn't want to face Pops. She looked at the lake, thanking her parents and

Souvenirs

Pops for keeping her away from him.ook. He was getting to be an expert on eggs easy over. orking to get Pops out of jail, and the Wilks were expecting the delive

Kara changed into her swimsuit, her mind buzzing as it chased ideas around one after another. She ran to the end of the dock and leaped into the water, letting herself sink before pushing with muscular legs to the surface. There was way too much drama going on for such a small town and her thoughts were too disorganized. She needed to sort everything out and get a better picture of what was happening before she could figure out the reason. She swam with strong strokes, pulling herself through the water.

rew the last stone with ht e er he is an accomplice to her face. The healthy lake enveloped her with its teeming life. She had been swimming in this lake since before she could walk. It had always been healthy thanks to her family.

She relaxed and floated on her back, delighting in the sun coming through the trees in shafts of light that played along the rippling surface of the lake along the shore. Further out, the lake seemed to gleam with millions of diamonds. She dove again into the cool water, scattering fish in every direction before rising to the surface.

The lake had been around so long, but was vulnerable and could be destroyed so easily. It was not a surprise to Kara that Mike would have so little regard for it. He didn't have any regard for others either. Why should he care about this little lake? He used everyone and threw them away like old candy wrappers. Why would a lake cause him any concern?

She dove again and stayed under the water. It rippled with sunlight and startled blue gills made bright reflections as they darted about. She loved this lake. Even in the winter the lake called to her. She loved to ice skate when the inlet froze over, go ice fishing or just sit on the dock and watch the snow fall.

The old family story told over and over was about Wea Indians who had protected the lake before a Dyer ancestor had wandered into the territory after the French Indian war. Now Pops protected this lake like generations of Dyer's before him. There wasn't anything noteworthy about it; it was just one small lake among all the lakes in the world. It may not matter that much in the whole scheme of things, but to the Dyer's, it was worth protecting. When her grandfather had told her she should be the lake's newest caretaker, she had immediately rejected the idea, but now she felt differently. She swam with even strokes to the dock.

Chapter 40

Harold had eaten breakfast at the diner and wandered over to visit with Walt. He was walking up Lewis Street as he returned to The Yellow Dog when he was almost run down by Blake, rushing from his office.

"Oh, Harold, sorry!" Blake held out his hand to steady the older man.

Harold laughed, "Where's the fire?"

"The hospital just called. Randy's starting to come to. I need to get down there."

Harold stood open-mouthed as he watched Blake drive away in the cruiser. He hurried to his truck to drive to the hospital.

He wasn't able to get anywhere close to Randy so he hung out in the café, drinking vending machine coffee while he waited.

"Harold?" Blake walked up to him.

"Can I buy you a cup of coffee, Blake?" Harold indicated a chair.

"I can't tell you anything; Randy hasn't come to yet, but the doctors think it'll be soon."

"Do they know whether he'll be okay or not?"

Blake bit his lower lip. "No way to know until he

wakes up."

Harold nodded. "Is it okay if I wait?"

Blake smiled and said, "I was going to try to call you anyway, but you refuse to carry a cell phone. I'm actually glad you're here because I need a favor from you. I'm supposed to interview a candidate early this afternoon for the deputy job, but, obviously, I need to stay here. If you could go meet with him, that would be a tremendous help. You town fathers are going to be talking to the guy I choose anyway."

Harold placed his hand on Blake's arm. "Let me get you some coffee before I head back to Monroe."

Blake grinned, "Decaf, okay?"

"Kara, that jerk just walked in." Wes pointed to Mike, who sat at the counter. "You're not allowed to kill him. Your mom wasn't happy about the little dinner theater you and Harold put on the other day."

Smiling, she walked out to the counter. "Well, look what the cat dragged in. What's your order?"

Wes motioned to Geneva, whose eyes widened when she saw Kara talking to Mike. She paled and turned panicked eyes at Wes.

Once again, Mike missed the signs others could easily recognize. "Hello, beautiful. I'll just take you since you look so good."

Still smiling, she retorted, "What about your casino and resort? The farm house is kind of small for something like that, isn't it?"

Mike's face darkened. "What are you talking about?"

Kara pulled the ad from her pocket. She'd planned on finding him today anyway and asking him about it. It was just good luck she didn't have to go to the effort.

"So what? I can do with it what I want. It belongs to me now and it's none of your damn business!"

Kara slammed the ad on the counter and grabbed his collar. "Wea Lake is my business. The people of Monroe are my business. So," she pointed to the ad, "this has become my business as well."

Mike tried to shake himself free, but the grip on his collar was too tight. "Nothing you can do about it, bitch!" He jerked against her hold. "Just because you drove trucks around for the army, you think you can take me on? You're just a dumb hick. You have no idea what you're up against."

Kara looked at him with a bland expression as she glared straight into his eyes. People who had been sitting at the counter moved away as Geneva and Wes converged on the pair.

"Kara Dyer, let him go!" Geneva's voice rang out. Kara didn't look at her mother, but she smiled as she released Mike. "Good thing someone's mommy is here to save you, little boy," she whispered tersely.

Mike's face twisted in anger as Wes sauntered around the counter. Mike growled before he stood up, smoothing his shirt.

Kara said lowly, "You're nothing but a dishonest jerk. I won't let you harm this lake or this community. You can take that to the bank."

Mike had turned to leave, but at hearing Kara's comment, he whipped around, his face once again a mask of rage. "What do you know? You're just a stupid whore!"

One of Bob's sons was suddenly standing beside Mike. Wes interceded, "Time to go, Mister. Your business is

Chapter 40

no longer welcome here."

Mike spat, "This is just a grease pit anyway," Glaring, he backed toward the door. Wes and Bob's son followed, watching until they saw his red coupe leave.

Bob's son grinned, "Can't let Kara have all the fun."

Geneva had pulled Kara into the kitchen. "Kara baby, go home."

Kara snapped her head up. Geneva reached out and touched her, realizing how tense her daughter was. Geneva rubbed her daughter's arms. "Kara, it's just a few hours until we close and things are a little slow. Go home; have a swim."

Wes had walked back into the kitchen. "Yeah, rest up because there will be a crowd tomorrow hoping to see another show."

Geneva glared at Wes.

Kara smiled. "Dinner theater."

Geneva's expression was so perplexed, Kara laughed and kissed her. "Okay, Mom. A swim sounds pretty good to me right now."

Souvenirs

Chapter 41

Kara drove the long way around the lake to go home. As she went through Monroe, she thought about what a lovely place this was to grow up. She could see how settling down in this close- knit community would appeal to people. She continued down the road. Most of the time you couldn't see the lake from the road, but Kara knew it was there, hidden behind the trees. As she rounded the south end of the lake, she slowed down and tried to imagine the Olson property developed by people who didn't care about Monroe or Wea Lake. She shivered at the thought. "No developer is going to get past me; not now, not ever."

When she got home she walked out to the dock where she sat on the edge, dipping her toes in. As she sat there, she thought, Monroe has gone along for years with nothing more shocking happening than kids getting drunk on Indian Island. She looked in the direction of Indian Rest Cabins. It seems like so many bad things have happened all of a sudden. First Hollis is killed then Randy is attacked. The Wilkes farm was destroyed by the tornado, which is just good old Indiana weather, but then Stan disappears. Kara's gaze shifted to the island. Oh, yeah, the drunk kids. She frowned. What happened to Hollis and Randy are

Chapter 41

connected. Kara kicked the water. Everything was going wrong this summer and it all started when Hollis came to town. No, wait, she thought. It all started with Stan.

She slipped off the dock, letting herself sink into the water. It was making her head hurt trying to piece all the information together. Rising to the surface, she let herself float. Gabe came into her mind, courting her with old-fashioned manners. She felt relaxed and fluttery at the same time as she replayed his last e-mail in her head.

Something else tickled her conscious thought like a dog scratching at the door. She tried to push everything except Gabe out of her head. That last communication from him was pulling almost all of her focus, but there was still that tickle, scratching and whining to be noticed.

She continued to float on the water as she reviewed his e-mail again. There was something Gabe had said about a summer resident. Her mind went over that thought. It was true most of the summer residents were old friends in the community. Some might even know about Bob's gun, but not what kind of rounds it required. The real problem was there would be no reason for them to kill Hollis, a stranger to everyone here, including the summer folk.

Her thoughts continued. She had learned Mike was attempting to develop the Olson property in a big way, but he didn't seem to be advertising in north central Indiana. The advertisement listed some corporation as the owner of the development and the property had just cleared probate. She thought, Mike would exploit a thing for all it was worth before casting it aside. Was he hiding behind a big corporation? No, Mike would want everyone to know what a big player he was. It's funny how he's trying to hide this.

Souvenirs

Why set up this shadowy secret business? She just couldn't see Mike sharing the glory with anyone.

Kara remembered the credit card he had tried using at The Blue Gill, and how Pops had commented that Mike should have taken her some place nicer. Maybe Mike's rich outward appearance, even his fancy leased car, was a front.

She also recalled how Stan had bragged about a big real estate deal. Was it the Olson Farm? But why would he take off?

The sounds of gun fire still echoed in her head. Guns. Her gun, Pops' gun, Bob's gun. Guns shooting.

She swam slow even strokes, letting her arms pull her weight through the water, her legs barely moving. She no longer felt the pull of the scars on her side. She dove again, her mind screaming at her in the water's cool darkness. Guns.

She suddenly remembered something; the membership card for a gun club falling from Mike's wallet. She recalled how he had always had a fascination for guns. One day Pops even caught Mike messing with the Nagant's display case. She recalled Mike's angry eyes just this morning and remembered his livid face being the epitome of the phrase, "if looks could kill".

Kara's mind sped up, her thoughts rushing in one after another. Hollis hadn't made it a secret that he wanted to develop affordable housing while protecting the environment; housing for working folks. Sure, he was interested in making money; he just didn't want to make a killing. "Killing" being the operative word.

Kara erupted from the water; silver drops suspended in the air. She felt as if she'd been hit with a lightning bolt.

Chapter 41

She flipped around, falling back into the water and allowing herself to sink. Was this the answer? Mike knows about the Nagant and the ammunition. He must have known about Bob's gun, too and could have broken into The Blue Gill when he was just a kid to check it all out.

She floated on her back while turning this theory over in her mind. Mike had found a way to disable Harold and prevent Hollis from building his affordable housing development. Mike knew Harold and Hollis were talking. The only other person who knew about their interchange was Stan.

Kara spun in the water, smoothly reversing her direction. She thought about Mike sleeping it off in his car at The Blue Gill the night Hollis was killed. Mike may have been able to break into The Blue Gill when he was just a kid. What if Mike hadn't been drunk the other night? He could easily have walked to Indian Rest, murdered Hollis, and walked back to The Blue Gill.

Another thought developed in Kara's head. Hollis's development would potentially make Mike's deal look unattractive to any business partners. She dog-paddled in the water. What would make Mike so desperate that he needed to kill Hollis?

Her eyes widened. Stan! Kara felt sick as the thought occurred to her: Stan is dead! He knew Mike was developing the property. Mike killed him, too! Kara swam for the dock as her mind shouted, Mike is running around loose!

It was Mike that Randy had seen walking back that night. She was sure of it. Kara barreled through the water to the dock. That day when Randy was out fishing, he must have seen Mike dump the Bears jacket he was wearing the night of the murder. Mike must have attacked him to shut him up. Why would Mike take such a risk? She knew it couldn't be for any other reason except self-preservation.

Did Mike need money that badly? Kara wondered. It would make sense and Mike and Stan weren't that much different in that regard. Cash was the key for both of them. Stan was always desperate to make money and Mike was always throwing it in everyone's face. She would need to talk to Blake about all this.

She swam back to the house and called him, but the dispatcher picked up. "Oh, Kara, Blake's not available right now. You want his voice mail?"

Kara sighed. "Okay." She waited for the voice message to finish then said, "Blake, this is Kara. I think I know who killed Hollis and tried to kill Randy. I think he might have killed Stan. I know the reason he tried to frame Pops and Bob. The only evidence I have is Mike Olson has a membership to an expensive gun club in Chicago. I saw his membership card on our one and only date, and he knew about the Nagants."

Kara hung up and walked back to the dock to dive back into the water. She had another thought, The beer on the island. Mike had been there! Mitch thought he heard zombies, but it must have been Mike roaming around in the woods.

The kids had gotten drunk on the beer Mike had probably left there. It was a good cover for his activities. Anything they heard or saw would be discounted because they were all drunk and it had almost worked. Perfect. A bunch of drunk kids wouldn't be believed. Mitch heard

Chapter 41

Mike, not zombies. Mitch saw and heard more than he realizes.

Kara jerked to a sudden stop.

Lord, have mercy! Mike didn't know the kids were going to the island. Mike hadn't planted the beer for the kids. It was for himself! He'd been watching the house!

She surfaced, her eyes going straight to the island. Kara knew Mike could have pretended to be drunk. A control freak like that would never allow himself to be so drunk in public as to be out of control. He got behind the bar somehow and took the gun and bullets from the ammo box. Bob never locked the case. The poor guy was always so trusting; it would have been easy for Mike to take advantage. He knew exactly where Bob kept that gun. He kept looking in the mirror the whole time we were there. Pops was right; he's such a dirt bag! Bob wouldn't have suspected anything. She pulled herself back onto the dock, shivering in spite of the hot sun. She walked upstairs, unable to shake the feeling of impending danger. She checked her gun to ensure it was loaded then turned to her computer.

That's what Stan meant by checking the listings, she thought. That isn't something she or anyone else she knew would do. However, a realtor would. Stan must have found out what Mike was up to.

Kara turned a scenario over in her mind. I can see Stan approaching Mike to try to get in on the deal. Mike must have panicked over Stan's alertness to the potential of making money off him. I bet Stan had hoped for a partnership with Mike in the development. He never could think farther than his wallet. Kara shook her head.

Mike found out about Hollis' plan to put in

affordable housing right next to his giant money-maker the night of their date. After all, the plans were all over the living room. Mike didn't want to fight Pops directly until he had to, but Hollis's development was going to screw things up for him. Kara now realized murdering Hollis was the only thing that was actually planned. Randy's attack was forced because Mike had lost control of the situation. Randy had thought the person he passed was Mitch and didn't have any idea he'd seen Hollis's murderer. Kara just couldn't be sure of Stan. For all she knew, he was just out of town. The disturbing thing was that another murder made sense.

Kara's stomach turned as she remembered Mike had found a dead "pig." Some poor guy even helped him throw the "pig" into the burn pit at the Wilkes'.

Chapter 42

"Well, young man, you're a big one, aren't you?" Pops said.

"Sir?"

"Our esteemed chief is away on police business so he sent me here to greet you. He's sorry he's not available. If you get selected, you'll be talking to us old guys anyway."

"Oh, well then. Nice to meet you, sir."

"Excuse me, Mr. Dyer, Blake is on the phone for you." The dispatcher spoke into the phone, "On his way right now, Blake."

Harold took the phone.

"What?" Harold had heard Blake. He just didn't understand what Blake was saying. "Kara?"

"Kara?" the young man said.

"Yes, Harold. I'm on my way to your place now. You need to keep Kara away. Randy's awake and he claims Mike Olson is the one who hit him. I knew he saw the killer on the road that night. I'm going to arrest Mike if I can get to him before Kara. You need to keep her out of the way. She's going to be furious and try to go after him. Mike Olson is dangerous. Understand?"

"Mike?" Harold's eyes reflected shock.

Souvenirs

"Yes, go get her and keep her in a safe place, okay? I'm telling you this because I'm afraid she'll hear about it. I'm trying to keep this under wraps, but it's probably already common knowledge. I don't want Kara killed and I don't want her charged with murder. I'm sure this news will be all over town in a few minutes."

Harold looked at the clock on the wall. "You're right. The diner's still open." He looked at his watch. "It'll be closing when I get there, but Kara should still be there." He ran for the truck. As he opened the door, the passenger side door opened and the young man he had just been talking to climbed in, saying, "I'm coming with you!"

Mitch had been helping his family with the temporary barn and Kara had decided to go to the Wilkes Farm to stand guard over him. She still couldn't shake the heightened awareness she was experiencing or the sense of danger she felt during her swim.

She didn't have any real evidence yet. She called and left another message for Blake. "Blake, I'm worried about Mitch so I'm heading over to the Wilkes."

She looked at herself in the mirror before leaving the house, remembering Mitch complaining she smelled like the lake. She decided on a quick shower before heading out.

The hair on the back of her neck continued to feel as if it were rising. She grabbed the gun from under her pillow and made sure there was a round in the chamber before she went to shower. She had felt this way before and had learned the hard way to follow what her gut was telling her.

After showering, she put on an old work shirt and jeans, pausing for a moment at a sound from downstairs. "Mom, you here?" She rewrapped the towel around her

Chapter 42

head and quietly walked down the stairs to look in the kitchen. Seeing no sign of her Mom, she continued on into the living room. She tensed; something was very wrong.

Chapter 43

Blake had driven to the Olson farm first but hadn't found Mike at home. After a quick search of the house, he left, heading up the road toward town. He dialed into his voice mail and heard Kara's first message.

"Oh, sweet Lord!" He hit the lights and headed for the Dyer's.

Blake passed what looked like Mike's car on the side of the road. He stopped and backed up. Yeah, there it was, mostly hidden. Blake called in his position, got out of the car and pulled his weapon. Scanning the tree line, he headed toward the car.

Mike had been watching Kara swim in the lake from the island. He thought, She is exquisite. The water made her hair darker, a stunning combination with her creamy skin. He admired her muscular, athletic build and perfect curves. Too bad she has such a smart mouth. He would make her respect him. I'll have her one way or another. He watched her leave the lake then rowed a skiff to cross from the island to the shore just west of the house. Before he could leave the tree line for the house, he saw Geneva drive up. Well, Mom isn't bad-looking for an old lady either. Maybe I'll take her, too then kill her in front of Kara. That would show that

Chapter 43

smart-mouthed bitch!

Mike saw Blake coming before Blake saw him, and took his shot.

Wes was the only one at the diner when Harold arrived. Lunch time had been slow that day and Wes had already shut down the grill.

"Wes, where's Kara? I need to find her."

Wes shot a look at the guy with Harold. "She left a while ago. Said she was going home. Why?"

"Randy has identified Mike Olson as his attacker, and he was definitely the person Randy passed the night Hollis was killed. Blake's gone after Mike. He wants me to sit on Kara."

"Oh no!" Wes covered his eyes with his hand. "Kara and Mike got into a fight over the land sale this morning. Mike was furious when we threw him out." Wes looked up at Harold in desperation. "I just sent Geneva home as well." The three men rushed out the door.

Geneva heard the shower running when she first came in. "Kara, I'm home!" She stood at the bottom of the stairs, listening, but Kara didn't answer. She went into the kitchen and had just taken a sip of iced tea when she heard the shot. A few moments later she heard a scuffle at the front door.

She walked down the hall and opened the door to find Blake and Mike. Blake was bleeding from his shoulder and had a couple cuts on his face. Mike was smiling and holding a gun to Blake's head. "Hello, Ms. Dyer. Is your daughter home? Shall we all wait in the living room for her?"

The first thing Kara saw was Blake, very still on the

Souvenirs

floor. He appeared to be unconscious and was bleeding from his right shoulder. He was handcuffed and there were dark stains on the rug trailing from the front door into the living room. Her dark eyes surveyed the room. Her mom was tied to a chair with duct tape over her mouth and Mike was standing in the middle of the room holding a gun.

"Well, the gang is almost all here. I don't suppose you know where Harold is by chance."

Kara shook her head.

"I was watching you from the island. Man, can you swim!"

"Watching me?" Kara's eyes darkened. "Why?"

"Look at you! Who wouldn't want to watch you?" He walked toward her and reached out to touch her, but she quickly moved away. "I would ask you to go back upstairs and put that sexy swim suit back on, but what you have on will do to start." He swept his eyes over her and said, "You don't have any lacy underwear, do you? I guess you wouldn't tell me even if you did." He grinned. "I bet you do. Maybe I'll go look after we're done."

Kara made eye contact with her mom as she continued to back away from Mike. "Mike, what are you doing?"

"Doing? At the diner, it sounded to me like you already know everything."

Kara moved towards Blake, but Mike blocked her, "No, no. You stay right there, sweetie."

"We need to get a doctor for him, Mike." Kara backed up towards the wall, palms out.

"Oh, he's not going to die. Yet. I just hit him over the head to keep him quiet. Even wounded, he was still trouble.

Chapter 43

Two-bit wanna-be Rambo. I had to shoot him. He just kept coming at me, but he's being a good boy now. I'll take care of him later." He leered at Kara. All her life, she had thought that smile to be so charming. Now it was just slimy. No wonder she was uncomfortable with him on their date. Some part of her had always known what Mike was.

"Mike, you don't have to do this."

"Yeah, Kara, I do. I knew you just wouldn't leave well enough alone. I don't know how you figured out I was broke. Did you find out I got my hand caught in the old office till? The old firm almost pressed charges against me. I had to borrow money from scary men to cover my little indiscretion. Instead of wearing cement shoes on the bottom of Lake Michigan, I had to sign over the family farm. Now I'm forced into being their front man. I need this deal to move forward or I'll be wearing those cement shoes. You just had to get in the way. This is your fault, slut."

Kara wasn't surprised by his statement about the money. She was stunned, however, by how deep he was in, but when had she voiced the assumption that Mike was broke?

Still pointing the gun at Geneva, he moved closer to Kara. "You do know you're the only girl in this flea bag town I haven't nailed. I ought to blow your Mom's head off just for that, but I have plans for her as well before I knock her off. I just wish Harold was here to see all this."

Harold was flying along the road for home when they passed Blake's car and spotted Mike's in the weeds. He hit the gas and drove faster.

Chapter 44

Geneva's eyes, the only part of her that could move, widened. Kara said, "Mike, you killed Hollis without any prompting from me."

He grinned. "That's right. You didn't goad me into it. It was pure luck I overheard that rather loud conversation at the diner that morning. Then that night, I saw the plans. Can you believe it? The project's right next to my little money-laundering franchise. I just couldn't have that. I thought no one would miss him out here. The blame would land on Harold or Bob by using that little war booty. Either way it takes Harold out of the picture." He glanced at the case. "You know that's what got me so interested in guns; his stupid Korean souvenir. Your grandfather never let me touch it. I devised the perfect plan. Harold would go to jail for murder and that would keep him from interfering with the development. I could rub Bob's do-gooder nose in it, and insure my silent partners stayed happy with me at the same time."

Kara fought her rising anger. "What about Stan?"

"Oh, come on Kara! You can't tell me you care a rat's ass about him. He was just a complete waste of air."

Kara knew she needed to keep Mike talking to

distract him. She was afraid he'd kill Blake or her mom. "Is Stan alive?"

"Was Stan ever alive?" Mike looked over at Blake.

Kara asked, "Did Stan find out about the development plans for your grandparent's property?"

"Kara, baby, this isn't what I would call foreplay. Don't you want to do something more stimulating?" He smiled at her again.

"Well, did he?"

Mike frowned, "Okay, if you like talking… yeah, Stan came to me with one of his 'deals.' He wanted us to go into a partnership. Now he's partnering with pigs." Mike laughed.

Blake moaned, causing Mike to turn toward him, but he kept his gun trained on Kara. He kicked Blake in the side, making him cry out in pain. Mike laughed again, "Good boy."

"So why did you try to kill Randy?"

"Randy. Damn him! I should have made sure he was dead. That dumb hick was everywhere." Mike waved his free hand. "He passed me on the road, and being a neighborly type of guy he offered me a ride, but I made sure he didn't see my face. Then when I was dumping the jacket, he was out there fishing, and again, being a good neighbor, he came rowing up to ask for a phone. It seems he found Stan's car at the bottom of the lake."

"So you hit him with the oar."

"Smart girl. He looked so stupid when the oar hit him, like some old dog." Kara remembered when Mike had shot at Rags. Rags wasn't hurt and Mike had claimed it was an accident, but Pops and her parents didn't believe him.

Souvenirs

Mike continued, "I thought he would be a vegetable. The name, 'Randy the Turnip' seems to fit him well."

He laughed again. "He was the only one who saw me. I would have made sure he was dead if I had the time. I was out in the open on the lake and didn't want to be seen by anyone. Then, of course, here comes pretty little Kara. You fished the turnip out of the water before I could come back and finish him off. I had to persuade a sweet little piece of ass who works at the hospital into watching him. She let me know when he woke up. She's so happy to do anything I want." He shrugged. "We take what we can get."

Kara was appalled. This guy was just plain evil. Kara said, "And you implied you dumped Stan's body in the burn pit?"

"Oh, very, very good. Stan was stupid. He wasn't going for the real money. He just wanted me to make him a partner or at least let him manage the property. I only advertised it to make it look on the up-and-up. I wasn't advertising it in this area because of Harold. My silent partners were going to buy it." Mike added, "Harold would find a way to interfere."

Kara could feel the anger boiling over in her. She looked at her mother's wide eyes and then down at Blake.

Mike continued, "So you could say Stan had to die because of Harold, so it's all his fault. If he had run off Mr. Affordable Housing instead of talking to him, this all would never have happened. I'm getting real tired of Harold interfering with my plans. Stan just couldn't figure out I didn't want people around here to know I was going to develop the property. I was trying to make it seem legit for my silent partners. As you discovered, my credit isn't

Chapter 44

exceptionally good. If people found out the money for the development wasn't coming from me, that wouldn't be good for my partners. Stan, the moron, never realized I killed Hollis. He thought it was just about the development of the land. I actually did everyone a favor. I was just making sure Stan's genes were removed from the pool, or were you looking to have Stan's kids?" He leered again at Kara.

Geneva grunted and Mike turned toward her. "Tried to keep her away from me, did you? You can't keep what I want away from me, don't you know that? You'll get your turn later."

Kara took a quick look at Blake while Mike's back was turned and noticed he was awake and moving.

Grinning, Mike turned back to Kara. She stiffened, pressing her back closer to the wall.

Mike said, "A man has needs." He grabbed at her and ripped open her shirt, sending buttons flying. He went from leering to staring, with his mouth open. "My God, what happened to you?" He indicated the scars. "Well, well, well. Good thing it didn't work out between us. I thought I would be compensated for marrying you by getting my hands on this property, and having a trophy wife would be an added benefit. Pretty arm candy. Glad I found out the truth now. Someone messed you up. So you're not as tasty as I had imagined. Damaged goods. Well, you're not going to be as yummy as I imagined, but I'll still take you anyhow. I win."

Mike turned again to Geneva, "Ms. Dyer, looks like I finally get Kara. She's just not as cherry as I would like." Geneva struggled and tried to speak against the duct tape.

Blake rolled over. Mike looked at Kara, following her glance. "Oh, coming to, are we?" Mike moved towards

Souvenirs

Blake, but still kept the gun pointing at Kara. "It might be fun to let him wake up and watch. Cops like to watch. Then I'll kill him."

Kara was no longer hearing what Mike said. She could hear her heart pounding in her ears. Time slowed down. She stepped away from the wall. Mike said, "Don't even think about it, you stupid little slut." Blake was struggling. "I think it's better if I kill him before we get started, Kara, don't you? He just might interrupt. We wouldn't want that, would we?" Mike turned to Blake, "I'm going to make you a hero, Blake, old boy. We can say you died in the line of duty, protecting Kara's virtue." Mike placed his foot on Blake's back and took aim at his head.

Time stopped. The only sound was the soft creak of the screen door blown open by the wind. Kara reached around behind her as the towel slipped off her head. Her hair hung in damp strands around her shoulders and her eyes burned with a deathly black flame.

Kara said calmly, "Pops isn't the only one to come home with war souvenirs. I guess you could call these scars mine." Mike turned to look at her, his eyes widening in surprise at the gun in her hand. "Since you were wondering what I had in my pants, I thought I'd show you. It's this little beauty. I got my souvenirs saving the good guys and killing the bad ones. As a matter of fact, I'm a war hero, you cry baby. Mikey, you're a bad guy." She fired her weapon, shattering Mike's elbow and sending his gun flying across the room. He screamed as he fell. She touched her scars and aimed the gun at Mike's head. "I brought these souvenirs home from the war, just like Bob and Pops."

"Mom and Dad were right. You're worthless. No one

is going to harm this lake or the people living here as long as I'm alive."

Mike, true to Harold's description, was sobbing. "They were going to kill me if I didn't make this deal go through. I owed them money."

Kara cocked her eyebrow, her eyes narrowing to black slits. "What in the world did you think gave you the right?" Mike looked up at her. Through his pain and terror he no longer even saw Kara. He was focused on his impending death. "Kara, please no, please! We were friends once."

"I'm not your friend. I never was. You don't have friends. You use people. You're the one corrupting the gene pool, Mikey. Time to get out of the pool." Dark, cold eyes regarded Mike as she leveled the gun at his head. "Good-bye, cry baby."

"Dyer, Stand down!"

Kara blinked.

"At ease, soldier."

Automatically, Kara moved her hands into a neutral position with the gun pointing up, and relaxed her stance.

"Kara, it's over."

A hand slid over her shoulder and then brushed softly against her cheek. "Girl, you can be scary."

The young man crossed the room in two strides and picked up a screaming Mike. "You saw! She was going to kill me! She's got some sort of war stress syndrome. She's crazy! You need to help me!"

The young man pursed his lips and shook his head. "You're mistaken. I don't help terrorists of any kind. At the top of that list are ones who irritate my girl." Gabe reared back and punched him in the face then let him crumple unconscious to the floor.

Gabe knelt beside Blake and helped him sit up, inspecting his wound. "That doesn't look too bad." He turned to Wes, who was freeing Geneva. He said, "Sir, you might want to call the medic."

Standing, he turned back to an open-mouthed Kara. "Surprised to see me? Didn't you get my letters?" Grinning, he walked toward his stunned comrade in arms, holding his hand out for her gun. Kara released the weapon and watched in silent amazement as he cleared the chamber, ejecting the clip. He then pulled her into his arms and kissed her.

Time started again. Gabe winked at Kara as he closed up her shirt. Turning to Blake he said, "You the local police chief?"

Blake nodded.

"I'm here for the interview."

For all those who choose to stand in
the breach for the rest of us, both on
foreign shores and at home.

Souvenirs

Sadly, Marsha's life path was hindered by being born a Chicago Cubs fan. Other than this disappointing genetic trait, she enjoys living along the coast of Maine with her wicked smart husband and ornery mother.

writer@marshahinton.com

www.ingramcontent.com/pod-product-compliance
Lightning Source LLC
Chambersburg PA
CBHW011512100726

47899CB00010BD/3336